Books in the American Dog series:

Brave
Poppy
Star

AMERICAN DOG
★ CHESTNUT ★

BY JENNIFER LI SHOTZ

HOUGHTON MIFFLIN HARCOURT
BOSTON   NEW YORK

hmhbooks.com

Produced by Alloy Entertainment

30 Hudson Yard
22nd Floor
New York, NY 10001

The text was set in Adobe Caslon Pro.

Library of Congress Cataloging-in-Publication Data is available.
ISBN: 978-0-358-10870-2 paper over board
ISBN: 978-0-358-10874-0 paperback

Manufactured in the United States of America
DOC 10 9 8 7 6 5 4 3 2 1
4500805201

For anyone who has ever told a dog a secret and felt a little better afterward

★ CHAPTER 1 ★

"Megan Lucille!" Meg's mom called from downstairs. Her tone told Meg that she had slept in long enough, even if it was her birthday. She could smell coffee and bacon and hot butter bubbling in the skillet. She heard the distant bustle in the kitchen as her sister and brother fought over the pancakes as soon as Dad flipped them onto the platter. Meg knew if she didn't get down there soon, they'd take all the perfectly golden ones. Sighing, she untangled herself from the warm flannel sheets, the heavy quilt, and the fuzzy blanket that wrapped her like a burrito.

She shivered as her feet hit the floor. She quickly found her fluffy robe and pulled on a pair of thick socks. Moving closer to the window, she saw that a crust of snow—maybe an inch or two—had fallen overnight. It sparkled like glitter in the morning light.

Grinning, Meg rushed into the bathroom to brush her teeth and hair. Ever since she was a little girl, she'd been convinced that snow on her birthday was good luck. Now that she was twelve, she was old enough to know it was a silly superstition, but even so . . . it couldn't hurt. Could it? Anticipation bubbled in her chest.

Meg caught sight of her frizzy brown bed head and sleepy face in the mirror. She took a deep breath and reminded herself not to get her hopes up. She pulled her hair into messy bun, then ran downstairs.

"Well, good morning, sleepyhead." Dad laughed as he slid a stack of two pancakes onto Meg's plate. "I thought maybe you were going to sleep all day."

Meg giggled, slathered a thick layer of butter on her pancakes, then drowned them in syrup.

Her older sister, Sarah, looked at Meg's plate and her eyes went wide. "Want some pancakes with that syrup, kiddo?"

Meg just smirked and took a huge bite. It was absolutely delicious. Just the way she liked it. "It's my birthday. You can have as much syrup as you want on your birthday," she mumbled through a mouthful of pancakes.

Sarah laughed. "Birthday or no birthday—we're going to need all hands on deck." She looked out the window. "Sunny days like this always bring the crowds." Sarah was seventeen and the coolest, smartest person Meg knew. She wanted nothing more than to be like her big sister when she grew up.

Their brother, Ben, groaned. "Maybe if we're lucky, it'll start to rain." At fifteen, Ben was slightly less cool and less smart than Sarah, especially since he was always teasing Meg and reminding her that she was the baby.

Sarah elbowed him in the ribs. "Tough luck. It said on the weather app it's going to be sunny all day. Which means . . . Say it with me, Ben."

Ben squeezed his eyes shut and tipped his head back. "Ugh. It means—"

"It's going to be a great day for trees," he and Sarah chanted in unison before bursting out laughing.

Meg watched her siblings and couldn't help feeling a pang of jealousy. She knew that her older brother and sister loved her, but they were closer to each other than they'd ever be to her. It was almost as if they spoke a secret language only the two of them understood, and they could crack each other up with barely a glance. Meg wanted to be part of the club. She wanted them to think she was just as hilarious as they were—and just as helpful, too.

Meg's family owned and operated a Christmas tree farm. They lived in a house on one end of their land and sold the trees from a lot at the front. Meg had been helping around the lot since she was little, but now that she was twelve, her parents were finally going to let her run one of the registers all on her own. Today was her first day, and Meg couldn't wait to get started.

Suddenly, her mom's hands slid over Meg's eyes, and she kissed the top of Meg's head. Meg could feel the rough calluses of her mother's hard work on her hands and smell the sap on her fingers. "Happy birthday, Meggie."

Her mom uncovered Meg's eyes and there, in the center of the table, was a box wrapped in red and green Christmas paper. It looked big enough to hold a toaster, and it had a bright silver bow stuck to the corner.

For a split second, Meg's stomach tightened with disappointment, then she scolded herself for being so selfish. She couldn't deny the truth, though: there was no way that box held what she really wanted. She'd asked for the same thing every birthday and Christmas for four years, ever since her best friend, Colton, and his rowdy but friendly dogs had moved into the house down the road.

But she'd come to realize that her parents would never get her a dog.

They'd had a family dog when she was a baby. His name was Bruiser. By the time Meg was born, Bruiser was very old. Her family had to scrape and save to afford his medical bills. Her dad was always saying that they would never get another dog because they were too expensive. But Meg suspected that her dad never actually loved Bruiser—not really. And with money being tight, the chances of getting a dog went from slim to none.

"Well, go on, then," Meg's dad said, using tongs to put another slice of bacon on Ben's plate. "Or are you waiting for next year to open it?" He winked at Meg.

She put down her fork, pushed her plate to the side, and tried a smile. She pulled the box toward her and ran a finger across the top of the bow. "Thank you," she said before peeling back the first piece of tape gently.

"Meg!" Ben laughed. "You are the slowest gift unwrapper ever!"

Meg scowled at him, but it quickly turned into a grin. "You know I keep the paper for crafts!" she said, taking her own sweet time. She liked that she did something that made Ben laugh, so she did it on purpose every time she opened a gift.

Her mom sat down on a stool and sipped her coffee. "If you don't like it, we can always return it," she said, watching Meg carefully. "I want to make sure that it's the one you like best."

Gifts were rare in the Briggs family, and even more so for Meg since her birthday and Christmas fell so closely together. She thought she might not even get a present this year. Only after she'd removed the paper without tearing it and folded it gently into a square did Meg lift the lid off the box.

Her breath caught in her throat. Her gaze fell upon a crisply folded, perfect new winter coat. It was bright purple with sparkling silver fur around the hood. Lightly, tentatively, she ran her fingers over the fur.

The last time she'd gone to the mall with Sarah, Meg had touched this same coat. She had imagined, for an instant, how cool she would look wearing it. But she never would have asked for it—it was too expensive, too frivolous. It was the sort of thing she couldn't truly imagine owning, even as it sat on her own kitchen table.

"Oh my gosh!" Meg exhaled, lifting it gingerly out of the box as if it would break. "I love it!" she said, standing up to try it on. "How did you know?"

Sarah laughed. "You made me go back to the same store to look at it four times, kiddo. I figured it was a pretty good guess. Do you like the color? Mom and I had a hard time picking between purple and blue."

"Yes, the purple is perfect!" Meg slid her arms into the sleeves and zipped it up, enjoying the tickle of fur on her cheeks as she pulled up the hood. Then she threw her arms around her mom, whose eyes were glistening as she looked at Meg. "Thank you, Mom. I love it, really."

Next, she hugged her dad. He wiped his hands on the kitchen towel before squeezing her back. "Happy birthday, Megs. I love you, sweetheart."

Meg stood on her tiptoes and kissed his nose. "I love you, too, Dad. Thank you."

She flashed a smile at Sarah and Ben. "Thanks, guys."

"Happy birthday, Meg. Your coat is awesome," Sarah said as she shoved her last slice of bacon into her mouth.

"Yeah, it's pretty cool. Happy birthday, Micro."

Meg frowned slightly but tried to keep her tone light. "Ben, could you . . . would you mind not calling me that anymore? I prefer Meg."

Ben had called her Micro ever since he learned that the word meant very small. Meg used to like it because it made her feel special. But as she got older, she realized that she secretly hated it for exactly the same reason. Nobody else had a silly nickname, but she had tons of them. Her dad called her Megs, and her mom called her Meggie. Colton called her Meg the Leg. But at least those were based on her name. Ben called her Micro just because she was younger and smaller than everybody else.

It was time they took her seriously.

"Sure thing," Ben said with a shrug.

Meg took the coat off carefully and sat down to finish breakfast, her mind purposefully trying to push away a feeling that nagged quietly at her under her excitement. It was guilt. Her parents must have scraped and saved to buy her that coat. She loved the coat beyond words—more than a million thank-yous could ever express. But there was also a pit in her stomach that she couldn't ignore. Her parents needed the money more than she needed the coat. She knew she should tell her mom to return it.

Her mom smiled softly as she held the tags at the end of the coat sleeve. "Well, if you're sure you like it, let's go ahead and cut these off." She pulled open the junk drawer. Meg drew a shuddering breath, knowing it was her last chance to do the right thing.

A sharp snip rang through the air as Meg's mom clipped the plastic tie. Then she threw the tags in the garbage, put the scissors away, and brushed her hands together briskly. "Well, that's that. It's all yours now." Meg smiled, awash with quiet, ashamed relief.

Her dad glanced at the clock on the microwave. "Oh, man. We've got to get to the lot. Gates open in twenty."

Suddenly, everyone burst into action, crisscrossing the kitchen and putting plates in the sink, finishing coffee, filling thermoses.

Her mom glanced at Meg, who was still in her bathrobe. "I'm sorry, sweetie. We have to get going, but we'll have a register waiting for you." She patted her on the arm. She knew how excited Meg was for her first day of real work.

In a blur of coats and boots being pulled on, her

family rushed out the door. It shut behind them with a thud. In the still quiet, Meg put the leftover pancakes in the fridge and took out a hard-boiled egg to bring with her for a snack later. She eyed her new coat draped over the back of a chair and wondered what the popular girls would say when they saw her in it after winter break. Would they want to hang out with her now? Would Colton be sad if she made new friends? As she wiped crumbs off the counter and into her palm, she thought about her best friend and knew the answer. He was too good and kind to be mean about anything. If she was happy, he would always be happy for her.

They had become best friends the minute they'd met, four and a half years earlier. He had moved into the house next to the tree lot in June, just after school let out. Her mom had heard from the mailman that the new neighbors had a son about Meg's age, and she had used that as an excuse to force Meg to go with her to meet them.

Meg and her mom had walked down the road, carrying a homemade strawberry pie covered in a thick layer of Cool Whip. Seven-year-old Meg had been desperately jealous, since strawberry pie was one of her favorite desserts ever, and her mom had only made the one. At the fence of the new neighbor's yard, they were met by a pack of barking, eager dogs, each one playfully clambering over the others, tails wagging as they begged for a scratch behind the ears.

"Oh, I . . . My goodness, that's a lot of dogs," Meg's mom had said, holding the pie a little higher.

Meg, however, had been in heaven. She had greeted each of them in turn, talking in a baby voice and giving them individual attention so no one felt left out. After a minute, she'd heard the front porch door slam.

"Come on, now," a boy's voice had called. "To me!" In a well-trained, perfectly executed move, all seven dogs turned and rushed back to the porch. "Down," the boy said, pointing to the ground. Obediently, the dogs lay down, lounging in the sun.

Meg had been instantly enthralled with the way the dogs listened so well, and she had smiled shyly at the boy. "Did you train them to do that?" she asked.

The boy shrugged, eyeing the pie in her mom's hands. "My parents helped, but . . . yeah, I guess so."

He finally met Meg's gaze. "I'm Colton, by the way." Then he looked at Meg's mom. "Hello, ma'am. My parents are in the kitchen, if you'd like to say hello." He looked back at Meg. "And I'll share that pie with you, if you want. Do you like playing chess?"

Meg quickly learned that Colton had two favorite things in the world: dogs and chess. He had been in his last school's chess club and everything. That summer was a whirlwind of playing with the dogs and Colton teaching Meg different strategies for winning at the board game.

Now they were best friends.

Meg couldn't wait to show off her new coat to Colton, whose favorite color was also purple. And she was eager to wear it for her first day at the register on the tree lot, too. Maybe, if she was very lucky, one of the kids from school would come to buy a tree, and she'd get a head start on those new friendships.

When she had gotten dressed and was finally ready to go, she pulled on a hat and mittens and stepped out in the bright, chilly morning. Outside, the sun peeked over the mountaintops, and the world sparkled with crunchy frost. The air stung Meg's lungs as she clomped across the yard, went around the barn, and opened the gate to the back end of the tree farm. Soldier-straight rows of Fraser firs spread out as far as she could see. The trees were perfectly spaced, as if an enormous hand had laid down a mile-long ruler before planting them.

Meg knew the best part of shopping at Briggs Family Tree Farm was walking through the rows, hunting for the perfect tree. Some families spent a whole day wending through the trees and debating the perfect height and width. As she walked along the end of the rows, she could see people already wandering around the farm—couples with two or three kids skittering around them, their breath clouding as they giggled and called out to one another.

In the distance, she heard a line from her favorite Christmas carol playing over the speakers at the front of the tree lot. The lyrics "chestnuts roasting on an open fire" floated toward her on the clean, crisp air. Meg's cheeks tingled with the cold, but she was warm and toasty inside her new coat. The breeze was heavy with the scent of needles and sap. Laughter rang out from all directions.

Everyone in the Briggs family loved Christmas, and Meg was no different. She had always thought that if people could see a Fraser fir decorated with nothing but ice and sunlight, Christmas would change forever. The stores would stop selling ornaments and strings of lights and start trying to recreate the magic of nature. It was so beautiful that for a moment, Meg stopped. She let all her senses absorb the sights and sounds and smells around her. Christmas gave her as much joy as her dad's pancakes ever did.

With sudden awe, Meg realized that her family's farm shared that magic with everyone who picked out a tree there. As a smile spread across her face, Meg felt the possibilities begin to grow around her. The spirit of Christmas lived here. Who knew what could happen?

★ CHAPTER 2 ★

Meg took the long way around the perimeter of the farm to get to the tree lot at the front of her family's property. The trees she passed varied in height from saplings to full-grown. The tallest ones stretched far over her head. Despite the frigid air, the sun shone down brightly, just as Sarah had predicted, and glinted off the frost-tipped boughs like diamonds. When she was little, Meg liked to imagine the gems had fallen to earth from the pouch of an unsuspecting giant.

This was the busiest season on her family's Christmas tree farm, when all their hard work for the last year paid off in a burst of a few short weeks. At least, it *should* pay off.

Meg sighed. Her family worked harder than anyone she had ever known. But even so, they had so many concerns. This year in particular was even more worrisome than usual. A long, dry summer had led to an infestation of spider spruce mites that had cost her parents a ton of time, money, and tree stock. The lost trees would take decades to replace. Her parents always tried to keep their problems quiet, but Meg had overheard them discussing bills, insurance claims, and other worries that made her stomach hurt to think about.

In fact, her dad had even talked about getting a factory job next year and closing the farm for good. When he talked about that, his voice got so sad and quiet that it was hard to hear him through the vents of their old farmhouse. Meg's dad's great-grandfather and great-grandmother had moved to North Carolina and planted Fraser firs on this land. This place was their family history, their legacy. To lose it would mean to lose some of himself.

Meg had no intention of letting that happen.

She was rounding a corner of the lot that no

customers had ventured into yet, and the field of trees stretched out ahead of her, empty and quiet. Her boots crunched in the snow. Of all the reasons Meg loved life on the farm, perfect, peaceful moments like this were her favorite.

Suddenly, between her footfalls, a strange sound broke the silence.

It was high-pitched—sharp and short. Meg scanned the tree line. Was there a family with a baby that she just hadn't seen nearby? She craned her neck and peered in every direction, but everything was still. Could it have been the wind blowing through the trees? But the branches were motionless.

I guess I imagined it, Meg thought.

She started walking but froze when she heard the sound again. This time it was unmistakably real. It was distant, off to her left, and it sounded desperate and sad—like whimpering, maybe. Meg took a few soft steps down a row of trees toward the sound, moving slowly and quietly. She listened intently.

The sound cut through the air every few seconds. The farther down the row she went, the louder it became. Meg knew she wasn't imagining the noise, and with every step it became clearer what she was hearing: the whine of a living creature. But what was it — and why was it crying out like that?

Her heart pounded in her chest, and she realized she was clenching her fists inside her gloves. What if it was a wounded raccoon or a coyote? What if the animal was dying? Biting her lip, she reached the end of the row. Meg was close. The sound was coming from just the other side of the last tree. She squatted down, took a deep breath, and pushed aside the bottom branches in order to peer through.

Her breath caught in her throat. A few feet away, she saw the wire fence that ran around the entire farm. There, stuck halfway through a large hole in the mesh, tangled in loose wire, was the source of the sound. Meg gasped and covered her mouth with her hands.

A brindled dog with dark brown and black stripes peered back at her with sad brown eyes.

They pulled her in, in an instant. She held the dog's gaze.

"Oh, you poor thing," she said. The dog whined in

response—a heart-wrenching cry for help. Meg moved toward him slowly, cautiously. The dog watched her, his eyebrows furrowed with fear and worry. "Shhh," she soothed him. "It's okay. I'm going to help you."

Meg almost couldn't believe what she was seeing. She had just been walking the route she always walked around the farm, and now this. Her birthday was turning out to be different after all. And hadn't she just been thinking about magic and possibility?

Meg reached the dog and dropped to her knees in front of him. The dog was shaking—from the cold and from his predicament—but he didn't flinch or growl at her. She held out a hand and let him sniff it. The dog gave her the once-over, then rested his head on her palm and looked up at her, his eyes pleading for help.

Meg held his head in her hand and ran a thumb over his snout. His fur was silky and smooth. With her other hand, she scratched gently behind his ears, just like she'd seen Colton do a thousand times. The dog let out a snort and wagged his tail.

"It's all right, buddy," Meg said. "I'm going to get

you out of there." The dog looked back at her as if he understood every word she said. Holding him steady with one hand, Meg lifted the wire from around his neck and unwrapped it from his body. He stayed perfectly still.

"What a good dog you are," she cooed. Meg untwisted the last loop from around him. He seemed too scared to move, so Meg put a hand on his shoulder and nudged him through gently. "Come on," she said.

The dog pulled himself through the fence, took a couple of stumbling steps, and shook himself out with a loud flap of his ears. He licked his side where the fence had dug into him, then looked up at Meg, as if to thank her.

"Are you okay?" she asked him, holding out a hand.

The dog sniffed her fingers and wrist thoroughly and then, after a moment, leaned into her, nuzzling her arm. His fur was icy and damp from the snow. How long had he been outside? The dog grazed her neck with his cold nose and exhaled sharply into her ear. She held in a laugh. After a moment, he stopped sniffing, nudged her once with his snout, and climbed right into her lap—his seal of approval. The dog raised his head and licked her chin. His tongue was rough, and his breath was puppy sour.

Meg giggled at the wiggling dog in her lap. Running a hand down his side, she felt his ribs jutting through his fur. He was so thin. His fur was soft, but tangled and matted with dirt, burrs, and brambles. The bedraggled sight of him brought tears to Meg's eyes. He had to have been on his own for a long time.

She couldn't imagine how such a cute, waggy dog would end up outdoors, alone—could someone have just left him out there, in the snow? It seemed impossible—who would do that? Maybe, Meg thought, he'd run away and gotten far from home. That made more sense.

The dog was busily licking at the pad of his right front paw, which was white, while the other three were brown and black. He jumped off her lap and raised the paw in the air. Looking up at her with his big eyes, he let out a sad little whine.

"What's the matter?" Meg asked, alarmed. "Can I see your paw?"

The dog limped back to her, and Meg held out her hand. Gently, sweetly, the dog placed his paw in her palm.

"Good boy," she said, lifting his paw to check the underside. "Are you hurt?" She saw the problem right away. One of the rough pads was cut and covered in dried blood, and one nail was jagged and torn. Meg winced. "You poor guy," she said soothingly.

It made Meg sad to think about, but it was clear no one had taken care of this dog in a long time. He needed someone to give him a warm bath, a clean bed, and a full bowl of kibble.

He needed someone to love him.

Meg's eyes filled with hot tears again in the cold air. She wanted so badly to be that someone.

She could see herself scrubbing the pup in the upstairs bathtub, then toweling him dry and snuggling with him on the couch. She pictured herself turning back to wave one last goodbye as he sat in the window and she headed off to school every morning. Her mind whirled with possibilities but always returned to one simple thought: she couldn't bring this dog home. She couldn't bring *any* dog home.

Her parents had been extremely clear that they did not want a pet. Every year she asked for a dog for Christmas, and every year her dad said no. She knew they'd be extra upset with her if she brought home not just a dog, but a dog who was lost, dirty, and injured. They would only see an animal that needed a lot of attention and expensive trips to the vet, not a sweet, lonely dog that just wanted to be loved. They would never say yes.

Meg shook her head and tried to push away any thoughts of keeping the dog. She stroked his cheek and rubbed the soft spot in front of his ears. He climbed back into her lap, closed his eyes, and let out a sigh.

But if she wasn't able to take him home, she thought as she gazed down at his face, what would she do with him? She couldn't just leave him outside in the snow, could she?

She couldn't help it—her mind began to spin with the possibilities again. Maybe her parents weren't against having a dog entirely. Maybe they just didn't want a dog who would add more work around the farm. But what if it was a really sweet, well-trained, totally obedient dog who didn't create more work but actually took some off their shoulders?

That was it! If she brought home a dog who could work on the farm, her parents would let him stay. Meg had a feeling that this little pup she'd found could be that dog—she just needed to get him cleaned up and housetrained, and maybe even teach him a few tricks.

Her imagination started to tug her in several different directions at once. She could train him to guard the farm. Or he could chase off the chipmunks her dad was always griping about, the ones that dug around the tree roots. Or he could be a tour guide on the tree lot! She and the dog could lead people around the farm and show them the best trees. And he could even sniff out the stragglers at closing time.

A useful dog would more than make up for the cost of his food, she figured. Just then, an image passed through her mind of her parents' faces, pinched with worry as they sat at the kitchen table with a collection of bills fanned out in front of them. Meg sighed and felt the dog's breathing grow slow and steady as he began to doze off in her lap. She watched his eyes flutter, and her heart nearly skipped a beat. He was so cute she couldn't imagine leaving him anywhere—and especially not out in the cold.

She had to try. Meg nodded to herself. She could do this. She would get him trained before she brought him home. And she would make enough money on her own to take care of him, so her parents wouldn't have to spend a dime.

The thought of money brought Meg's mind screeching back into the present. She realized she'd been sitting there on the frosty, hard ground with the dog for a long time. Her family was expecting her at the office —she had to get moving before anyone began to wonder where she was. But first she needed to take care of his wound.

Meg eased the dog off her lap. He rolled onto his feet, his injured paw slightly elevated, with his tail up and wagging. When she stood up, he leaned his whole body against her leg. Then he pushed his head into her hand, demanding a scratch behind the ears. She was happy to oblige. Meg knelt down and took his face in her hands. They stayed like that for a second, nose to snout, staring at each other. His warm dog breath wafted around Meg's face and she smiled.

Her chest nearly burst with the thought of keeping him. She would put her plan into action right away. She just had to figure out where she could hide him while they got started.

Meg was so excited she bounced up and down on her toes a little. This dog was the best secret of her entire life. Her birthday just kept getting better and better.

"Come on, boy," she said, starting off down the row of trees. "Let's find someplace to keep you warm. I need to figure out how we're going to make this work!"

As if he knew what she was saying, the dog trotted along beside her. He limped on his front leg just slightly, but he stuck close to Meg and let out a happy yip.

"You're a good boy," she said. "And if we work together, you're going to be mine."

They fell into stride, and the dog seemed perfectly

willing to trust her to take him where he needed to go. Grinning, Meg began to whistle. The sun was shining, the birds were singing, and her dog was walking beside her.

★ CHAPTER 3 ★

Meg found herself by the old, abandoned shed near the edge of the farm. Her dad had stored farm equipment in it until they built the second barn, which was bigger and closer to the main office, when Meg was five. This shed was rickety and weathered. Her dad had talked about tearing it down several times. But thankfully it was still standing. And right now, it was a perfect hiding place for an injured dog.

"Come on, boy," Meg said, patting her thigh as she tugged on the door. She had to pull hard to get it to open even a little. The door creaked, its rusted hinges squealing with disuse.

Meg's eyes took a moment to adjust to the dim

light broken only by strips of sunlight that burst through cracks in the wood. Dust mites danced in the air, which smelled of old, musty straw, rust, and dried fir needles. The shed wasn't the most welcoming place, Meg knew. She sighed. She wouldn't want to be stuck in here, that was for sure, but this was the best idea she'd come up with so far. She fumbled around until she found the pull-string for the light. Amazingly, it still worked after all these years.

The dog stepped forward hesitantly, sniffing at the air with curiosity. After a long moment, he looked up at her with an expression of confusion. He lowered his nose to the ground and sniffed his way deeper into the shed. He made a quick study of the perimeter, then returned quickly to Meg's side and sat down at her feet. He whimpered and pawed at the ground. She felt him shaking against her leg.

His obvious fear was making Meg feel awful, and she couldn't blame him. The shed was old and stinky, and even if it wasn't scary, who would want to spend a beautiful day like this stuck inside? But she couldn't take him with her, and she couldn't risk him running off. If she was going to give him a good home, he was going to have to be patient—they both were.

Meg took a breath to steel herself. She knelt down and patted the dog's head. "It's just for a little while, I promise," she said, trying to sound more confident than she felt. He waggled his tail and planted a wet, happy kiss on her cheek. Meg laughed. "I have to go to work." She sighed. "But I'll come back tonight and take you to see my friend Colton. He knows everything about dogs. He'll help me get your foot better and figure out what to do next. Okay?"

The dog listened intently, his gaze never leaving her face.

"And once I get you cleaned up and trained a little, you'll come home with me," Meg said, grinning. The dog responded with an eager, expectant yip. His whole rear end swayed back and forth with his tail. "Before I go though, you need a name. What should I call you?"

She studied his beautiful brindle coat. He didn't look like a Duke or a Charlie or any of the usual dog names. Plus, she wanted it to be something special—something that reminded her of the moment she first found him. Meg thought back on the morning: the pancake breakfast, her new coat, the rows and rows of Fraser firs, the magic of her birthday and the tree farm, "chestnuts roasting on an open fire" playing over the farm's speakers.

A beam of sunlight crossed the dog's back, making his brown and black coat look velvety and richly colored. She squinted at him. His fur reminded her of something . . . it took her a second to place it. Finally she had it, and a smile crossed her face. He was the same color as her favorite holiday snack, a treat her family loved to share around the fire at night: a chestnut.

"Chestnut!" She grinned, scratching his ears and crooning to him. "Is that your new name, buddy? Are you Chestnut?"

The dog barked happily and did a little skittering dance with his front paws, which Meg took as a sign of approval. She patted him on the side and realized that under all of his playfulness, he was still shivering.

"Oh, no! Are you cold?" She looked around the shed for something she could use to make a bed for him. There was nothing but a few scraps of wood and some loose pieces of straw strewn across the ground. What was she going to do?

But before she could solve that problem, a loud gurgle erupted from Chestnut's tummy. Meg felt terrible—it hadn't even occurred to her that if he'd been stuck outside on his own for a long time, he was probably hungry.

Her snack! She pulled the hard-boiled egg from her pocket and quickly peeled it for him. Chestnut took it from her palm and gobbled it down. When he was done, he let out a contented snort and licked his snout. Now Meg just had to figure out how to keep him warm.

She looked down at her own outfit and swallowed hard. There was one thing she could do.

Meg unzipped her new coat hesitantly. The fabric made a soft *whoosh* as she pulled her arms from the sleeves, and a blast of cold air brushed against her face. Now that she was just in her sweatshirt, she felt a chill. Her new jacket had been keeping her so warm

—she couldn't imagine how cold Chestnut must be. That strengthened her resolve. She was doing the right thing.

"I'll leave this for you until I can get you some blankets," she said, wrapping the coat around the dog's body. She tried not to wince at the thought of how much it had cost her parents. "This will keep you nice and warm." Meg stood up and gazed down at the sweet, shivering pup under a huge purple coat, with just his head sticking out. Chestnut looked back up at her with a furrowed brow—like he knew she was leaving and he didn't want her to go. "I'll be back really soon," she said. "In just a few hours."

Meg glanced at her watch and gasped. She hadn't realized how long she'd been with him. "I've got to get to the lot—I'm so late!" She spun on her heel and headed to the door of the shed, the swaddled dog limping after her. "Stay!" she said as she slipped through the door. With one last look at his confused face, she closed and latched it behind her before he could get out. Chestnut immediately started whining and scratching on the other side of the splintery wood door, which shuddered against Meg's hand. He barked frantically, then let out a howl that nearly broke Meg's heart.

"Shhh, Chestnut," she whispered. "Shush! It's going to be all right. But you have to stay here!"

Again, the door shook. His barks and whines got louder and more persistent. The sound poured through the gaps in the flimsy walls and rang out over the fields. Meg worried that her parents would hear it, even as far away as the lot.

"Okay, buddy, please stop," she pleaded. She unlatched the door and stepped back into the dim space. Her coat lay discarded on the ground, and Chestnut trembled anxiously at her feet. She sat down next to him and tried to get him to settle down, petting him softly and shushing him like a parent would a newborn baby. For a few long moments, he tapped from one paw to the other, scratching at the dirty floor and looking at her intently. Meg tried hard not to worry about what time it was.

She rubbed him behind the ears until he finally lay down with one last, high-pitched whimper. He seemed drained.

"Let's try again," Meg said in a gentle tone. She slowly got to her feet, still leaning over and continuing to pet Chestnut's head. Keeping a hand on him, she took one backward step toward the door. His ears instantly shot up and he jumped to all fours, his tail standing straight up. He let out a stream of barks so loud and intense that it hurt her eardrums.

Meg froze in her tracks. She sat back down on the ground and began to soothe him again. After a few minutes, they repeated the process. Meg stood up and kept a hand on the dog, then tried to leave. The next time she made it two backward steps toward the door, then the time after that she made it three. It felt like forever, but after several tries, Meg stood in the open doorway looking down at the little dog. He shook nervously but didn't bark. She stepped backwards into the snow and put a hand on the door to pull it shut.

"That's a good boy!" Her voice came out higher

pitched than she'd intended it to. "That's it, Chestnut. Goooooood boy."

She eased the door shut and held her breath as he heaved his body against the other side. It was awful to think of him being that upset, but Meg took a deep breath through her nose and exhaled slowly through her mouth. It was a trick her sister had taught her when Meg was younger and would get mad about a broken toy or playground slight.

Chestnut began to whimper and bark, but it was calmer—and quieter—than before. Meg sat down on the cold ground and leaned back against the wood.

"That's it, Chestnut," she cooed through the cracks. She heard him scuttle around inside, as if he were getting ready to lie down. He let out a little snort, letting her know that even though he wasn't making as much noise, he definitely still wasn't okay with the situation.

"You're doing great, buddy," she said through the door. He grunted in response and scratched at the wall, then grew quiet. Meg took that as a good sign. She stood up and brushed the dirt and snow off her pants.

She took a couple steps without hearing any reaction from the dog. But when she got a few feet away, her boots crunched loudly in the snow. She winced and stopped in her tracks, waiting. Sure enough, Chestnut went crazy, barking and howling, terrified of being left alone.

A moment later, Meg found herself sitting on the ground inside the shed again, running a hand over the anxious dog's smooth fur. She was starting to get really stressed about getting to the lot. What would she tell her parents?

"Listen, Chestnut," Meg sighed. "I know it stinks to have to stay in here, but I promise you—it's just temporary. Just until I figure out what to do with you."

He let out a little disgruntled snuffle and rolled onto his side, keeping a stern eye on her.

"And then I have to prove to Mom and Dad that I'm responsible enough to keep you. But being late for work on my very first day isn't going to help me at all." Meg had heard countless parents trying to reason with their kids when the little ones wanted a tree that was way too big for their house, and she'd heard the difference between success and frustration. She knew to sound firm. "I've got to go, buddy," she said.

At the change in her voice, Chestnut glanced up at her, his eyes wide with fear. "But I promise, I'll be back as soon as I can to take care of you. I'll get you more food and some water. I'll bring Colton to help me with that foot, okay?" She scratched at his belly until he rolled onto his back, wiggling happily. Meg's guilt subsided a little. "But you've got to let me go, or else none of that will matter."

Chestnut held her gaze for a long moment, then something in his expression changed — almost as if he understood exactly what she was saying. He let out a deep, accepting sigh and looked up at the ceiling. Meg saw that his eyelids were starting to look heavy. He must have been exhausted after all the excitement of the morning, Meg thought.

She patted his belly more and more softly, until he put his head down on the ground and his eyelids began to sag. Meg covered him with her coat again. Chestnut tucked his chin and rested a single paw over his own nose. Then his eyes slid closed in slumber.

Relief washed over Meg, and she glanced toward the door. She had to sneak out before Chestnut woke up. She stood up slowly, silently, trying not to rouse the dog. Chestnut's legs twitched beneath her coat, and he made a funny little dreaming sound. Colton had told her once that dogs were often calmed by the scents of those they loved and trusted. Her coat was new, but it probably already smelled like her.

Tears sprang to Meg's eyes. Chestnut already needed her.

And she loved him more than she could explain.

Chestnut's eyes stayed closed. His breathing grew slow and steady, and her coat rose and fell with his chest. Meg pulled the door closed as quietly as she could and latched it behind her.

Back in the crisp morning air, Meg blinked a few times. Her birthday had taken such an unexpected—and exciting—turn. She studied the shed, almost as if she were trying to figure out if everything that had just happened was real. Just then, her gaze fell upon a beautiful, perfectly symmetrical pinecone lying on the ground to her left. She hadn't noticed it before.

"Whoa," she whispered. She stepped over and picked it up to examine it. Her mind began to whirl with ideas, and as she began to formulate a plan, a huge smile broke out on her face. It was perfect!

Just a few days earlier, Meg had been online searching for new Christmas tree ornaments, and she'd seen some beautiful hand-painted pinecones. She'd loved them—and now maybe she could make them herself. What if she painted the pinecone? What if she made something so pretty that people would want to buy it? If she sold enough of them, she might be able to use the money to keep Chestnut.

The thought made her heart pound.

Meg stuffed the pinecone in her sweatshirt pocket and traced the edges of it with her fingertips. As she headed away from the shed, her mind thrummed with her business idea. But as she turned back to glance in Chestnut's direction one last time, she realized that she had another problem.

She didn't know a lot about dogs, but she knew that Chestnut was really anxious—and that level of anxiety wasn't normal. Colton had a dog once that got so stressed out when the family was away that they had to rehome it with a retired man who was home all day.

Meg wanted a dog more than anything in the world, and she was already getting attached to the idea of Chestnut living with her forever. But she couldn't ignore the fact that a mountain of problems was piling up in front of her—and getting taller by the minute. She didn't know how to overcome it all.

The pinecone pressed into the palm of her hand and she drew in a deep breath. She could still feel the warmth of Chestnut pressed against her leg as he slept. She could still smell him, and she smiled. It didn't matter if her problems were as tall as Mount Everest. Chestnut was worth every bit of effort. Meg vowed that she'd work as hard as she had to, for as long as she had to. And she didn't have any time to waste.

As she raced back to the house to grab her old coat before sprinting to the tree lot, she let herself make plans as if all her dreams depended on them. Because, she thought, they just might.

★ CHAPTER 4 ★

All the big ideas swimming around in Meg's mind slipped away when she realized just how late she really was. As she ran toward the lot, all she felt was shame.

This was her first day ever working the register, and she had wanted so badly to make a good impression, to prove to her parents that she was ready for the responsibility—not that she was forgetful and immature.

To make matters worse, for the first time in her life, she had a secret to hide from her parents. A big secret.

She couldn't believe how busy the tree farm already was. A line of impatient customers snaked from the registers toward the rows of trees. Her mom was punching numbers into a register with an expression that didn't convey too much holiday cheer. An annoyed-looking customer stood silently, waiting to finish paying. Meg slid behind the counter and took an apron off the hook.

"Where have you been, Megan?" her mom asked without looking up, her words clipped but her tone bursting with frustration. "You know this is a two-person job, and you've been begging to help." She handed some change back to the customer and smiled, though it didn't quite reach her eyes. Meg saw that her mom's ungloved hands were raw with cold. She couldn't wear gloves and make change, Meg knew. And this was just the start of the day—they'd be outside for hours.

"You folks have a very merry Christmas," Meg's mom said to the customer. "And thank you so much for your patience." The man nodded and left, and the next customer rushed forward, her credit card in hand.

Meg dropped the thick canvas apron over her head and tied it around her waist. Her old coat was bulky underneath it and she fidgeted, trying to smooth everything into place. "I'm so sorry, Mom. I guess I just lost track of time."

And since she couldn't tell her mom the *real* reason she was late, Meg turned and gave a chipper wave at the family that was approaching her register.

"Did you folks find what you were looking for?" Meg asked. She hated lying—and she hated disappointing her mom. She was already on the verge of tears, but she was determined not to mess up again. So she put on a pretend smile and did her best to enter the charges into the register correctly.

Cheerful holiday songs played over the speakers, while in the distance, a chainsaw did its work on someone's chosen tree. One of the farm staff was busy loading a basket with green and red Christmas-tree-shaped sugar cookies, while another mixed more steaming cocoa into a large urn. Sarah was zipping around rearranging wreaths and garlands that had been moved by shoppers. A four-wheeled ATV buzzed past, and Ben waved goofily from behind the handlebars.

Meg had waited her whole life to work side by side with her family—to be a part of the family business

—but suddenly, she didn't want to be there. The thought made her feel so guilty that she could barely focus. She wished, instead, that she was back in the shed, snuggled up with Chestnut under her coat. At least there, she wouldn't disappoint anyone. Her mom's hard frown did nothing to make her feel any better, either.

The family at the register was laughing as the mother paid for their tree and garland. Mr. Mike, who'd been working for her parents since before Meg was born, hauled the family's tree to their minivan and placed it on top like it was feather-light. Meg watched as the oldest son helped him tie it down with twine.

"Your family grows the most beautiful trees," the mother said, smiling warmly at Meg. "It must be like a Christmas dream, growing up here."

Meg smiled so hard her cheeks hurt. "It is," she said, a little too loudly.

The mother looked over her shoulder at her own children, then said, "And your parents must be so proud of you, working so hard. My own kids don't know how lucky they have it."

Meg's smile wavered, but beside her, her mom said, "We are very proud of all our children, ma'am. Thank you so much."

Meg didn't dare look at her, for fear her mom would see a lie in her eyes.

After a few hours of nonstop rushing to help their waiting customers, counting out change, and wishing a thousand merry Christmases, there was a brief lull. Meg's mom looked at her, her eyes still flashing with irritation at her daughter. "Where's your new coat?"

Meg's heart hammered in her chest. Had she made a terrible mistake leaving it with Chestnut? What if he chewed it up or tore a hole in it? The pancakes in her stomach turned sour as she prayed her expression looked innocent. "I didn't want to get it dirty, so I left it at home," she said.

Her mom nodded, as if it was the first reasonable thing Meg had said all day. Too bad it was a lie. Meg felt awful. She was disappointed in herself that she had nearly blown it when her family had finally trusted her with a little responsibility. And now, she was terrified that she'd left her new, expensive coat to be ruined by a stray dog that her parents would never let her keep. She was nearly overcome with guilt. Chestnut was worth the risk, but Meg didn't like the way she felt at all.

"I really am sorry, Mom," she said, shoving her hands into her pockets, where her knuckles grazed the pinecone she'd picked up earlier. "I was . . . I was out picking up pinecones." She pulled it out of her pocket to show her mom. "I thought maybe we could do something special with them. Maybe we could sell them —here at the register. Do you think people would buy them?"

Her mom sighed. "I don't know, Meggie."

Meg tried not to cringe at the sound of her nickname. Would her mom ever stop calling her that?

"Maybe . . ." her mom went on, her face softening. She pulled Meg into a hug. "What were you thinking?"

And just like that, Meg knew that her mom wasn't quite as mad at her. She never did stay mad at Meg for very long. Ben said it was the benefit of being the baby of the family, but right then, that just made Meg feel worse.

For the moment, though, Meg would take her forgiveness. The rest she could prove later. "What if we made ornaments?" Meg said, getting excited. "There's so many pinecones left lying around. And they're free —we'd just need paint and glitter and—I don't know!"

Her mom smiled at her enthusiasm, her tired eyes lighting up a little.

Just then, Ben walked by and overheard their conversation. "What do you know about pinecones, Micro?" he asked teasingly.

Meg rolled her eyes. "I know that every summer, we pull off about a million of them from the trees," she said.

Her mom nodded, her eyebrows pulling together in thought. "We do that to help conserve the trees' energy while they're—"

"Growing, I know," Meg said.

She knew exactly what her mom would say next. This was the same speech they gave when school groups took tours of the farm. "It helps the trees grow bigger and have lots of room for ornaments," Meg said, shooting Ben a sharp look.

"Okay, okay," Ben replied with a shrug. "So you know all there is to know about pinecones." He walked off to help a customer.

Meg's mom raised her eyebrows, clearly impressed at Meg's knowledge.

"Then, in late summer," Meg went on, "the barn is filled with pinecones that we harvest new seeds from."

The seeds were used to plant the next generation of Fraser firs, which was one of Meg's favorite parts of working on the tree farm. The seeds grew into tiny saplings in the greenhouse. Then, once they got big enough, her parents and siblings and the farm staff planted them in long rows.

"When did you learn all that?" Meg's mom marveled.

Meg shrugged. "I don't know, I just did. And I know that there are millions of pinecones all over our land that I can use to create some really pretty ornaments."

She looked at the ground, suddenly embarrassed. "And if it's okay with you, I'll try to sell them to the customers here at the lot."

And maybe, just maybe, the ornaments would sell well enough to help her convince her parents to let her keep Chestnut.

As another family approached the register, Meg's mom reached over and tucked a loose lock of hair behind her ear. "I think it's a great idea, Meggie, and every little bit helps."

The rest of the day flew past. Meg was so busy handing out change and holiday wishes that she lost count of how many trees she sold. The long weekend after Thanksgiving was always one of their busiest times of the season, and this year was no exception. After a few hours, her nose was so cold she thought it might have turned permanently red.

Still, Meg's mind was only partly at the tree lot. As she refilled the cookies and checked the hot cocoa dispenser, a part of her was curled up with Chestnut in the shed. And yet some of her mind was also busy designing all the ornaments she would make to be able to keep him.

She was delirious from the hard day's work, but Meg didn't even care about the cold. Her imagination was too busy overflowing with ribbons and beads, paint, glitter and glue.

★ CHAPTER 5 ★

When the long workday had finally come to an end and the last tree-shopping family had pulled out of the lot singing Christmas carols and planning the perfect holiday, the Briggs family straightened up the register area and swept the loose needles into piles. Meg was organizing the wreaths, but her mind was already wandering back to the shed with Chestnut. He was hurt, and he must be starving. She had to get to him. As the sun slid lower, Sarah, Ben, and Meg's mom and dad headed toward the truck.

"Coming, Micro?" Ben hollered.

Meg shook her head. "Is it okay if I run down to see Colton for a minute, Mom?" she asked, trying not to look as excited as she really was. "He asked if I could come over."

Her belly twisted guiltily at the lie — her second of the day — but her mom just nodded tiredly. "Of course, honey. If you need a ride home, just give me a call."

As the rest of her family climbed into the truck, Meg's dad rolled down the window. "Don't stay out too late, Meggie. We've got another busy day tomorrow. It's supposed to be even nicer than today."

"I won't, Dad. I promise." Meg pulled her hat down over her ears, then raced down the road to her best friend's house, certain that he would know how to help Chestnut.

At the edge of Colton's property, Meg was met by a herd of joyfully energetic dogs that wiggled and bumped against each other as they fought for her attention. She stopped and petted them all, calling each one by name and letting each of them lick her face in greeting. "Oh, good girl, Tinker," she said, scratching an Australian shepherd's neck. "Who's a good boy, Winston?" She rubbed the belly of the little Jack

Russell. "Want to shake, Charlie?" she asked, holding her hand out for the gray-muzzled lab. "Good dancing, Jack and Jill." She giggled at the two mixed-breed dogs that spun in circles, vying for her ear rubs. The retired greyhound, Baron, walked slowly up to her and sat regally. Meg knelt in front of the aged animal and scratched under his chin. He nuzzled his warm, wet nose into her hand.

"What's going on out there?" Colton shouted from inside the screen door. "To me," he commanded, and every pair of canine ears perked up before the entire crew charged off toward him as one. Meg was left alone at the edge of the yard. "Hey, Meg!" Colton called out once she was unburied from the pile of fur and affection. "What are you doing here?"

"Hey, Colton," she said, following after the dogs.

"What's up?" Colton asked. The Christmas lights in the yard flicked on, illuminating her as she approached.

Colton stepped out onto the porch and ran a hand over the top of his hair. Ever since he'd decided to grow his hair out on top, he was always trying to fix it into place. Meg giggled. "You just making sure it's still there?" she asked.

He pulled on a pair of muddy boots that sat on the stoop and grimaced at the cold. "A man's fade has got to be in perfect order," he said, grinning broadly as he trotted down the steps to meet her. "Hello, beasts." He ruffled the fur of his four-legged friends, who had gathered at the bottom of the steps and watched him attentively.

Colton then held out a fist toward Meg, which she bumped with her gloved hand. "Happy birthday, Meg the Leg." He'd started calling her that on the first day she met him, when he had just moved to their school and she had scored a goal in gym class soccer. These days he only brought out the nickname for special occasions.

She beamed at him, taking in his generally rumpled appearance and wide smile. "Thanks, Colt. I need a favor, though."

"What's up?" he asked again. He picked up a stick from the ground and threw it for the dogs to chase.

Several tore off after it, while the older ones huffed and lay down, happy for the moment of relative calm in their lives—and the scratches Meg and Colton offered.

"I . . . uh, I found a dog," she said, feeling suddenly shy about her plan. Saying it out loud meant it really wasn't something she'd dreamed or made up. It was real. Chestnut was real.

Colton's eyes went wide. "What? Where?"

"On the farm. He was stuck in the fence—he's so cute, Colt. You wouldn't believe him!"

Just talking about Chestnut made all her shyness disappear. She was so excited to tell her friend everything about the dog that the words came tumbling out of her mouth. She told Colton about untangling Chestnut from the fence and taking him to the shed and spending so long trying to convince him to stay there while she went to work. She described how the pup had acted when she'd tried to leave, how he'd seemed afraid and anxious. Meg watched Colton's face carefully for any hints to how he was reacting. What he thought about Chestnut would tell her a lot about the dog—and her chances of keeping him. After all, Colton was the son of the county's two best veterinarians. He knew everything there was to know about animals, and dogs in particular.

But Colton was just listening carefully and not displaying any response one way or the other.

"He's pretty skinny," Meg went on. "And his paw is hurt. He's limping a little, but if I could get him healed and cleaned up, then I could train him and maybe my mom and dad would . . ."

She glanced at Colton, who had started biting his lip and staring at the ground, like he was lost in thought. Meg knew that look. It was the same one he got when he was thinking about the next move in a chess game. Her gut twisted with worry. If Colton wouldn't help her, she didn't know what she'd do.

"Why do you look like that?" she asked nervously. "You think it's a bad idea?"

"I'm not saying that." He shrugged. "I'm just thinking about everything you've told me about your parents and dogs, and, you know, they don't sound like they'd be into it at all. Do you really think your folks are likely to let you keep him, no matter how well trained he is?"

Meg winced. One of the things she loved most about Colton was his honesty, but that didn't mean it wasn't hard to hear sometimes. He had a kind heart and a ready smile, and they had an unspoken deal as friends: always tell the truth. And Colton was right.

"I know, but—" Meg didn't know how to finish the sentence. Wanting her parents to change their minds wasn't going to make it happen. Her heart sank, but then she stopped herself from giving up. All day, Meg had been imagining the scene of her parents meeting Chestnut and being won over by his cuteness. In her mind she'd seen them saying yes, and she wasn't going to let go of that without a fight.

"I just worry that showing up with a dog is the last way to get them to change their minds," Colton said. "It might make them feel kind of . . . I don't know, pressured?"

"But what if they did? Change their minds, I mean."

Tinker came running back to Colton with the slobbery stick in his mouth. Colton took it and hefted it in his hand.

"That'd be great," Colton answered, hurling the stick across the yard again. The dogs shot off after it with a clatter of claws and yips. "But, Meg, think of it like chess. You have to consider every possible move and think three steps ahead. What're you going to do if they don't?"

Meg understood what Colton was trying to say. Truthfully, she should've expected this practical answer from her best friend, but she didn't have time for his skepticism. Besides, thinking three steps ahead was what she was *trying* to do by asking for his help.

Meg shook her head. "I'm not going to think about that yet. Let me worry about my parents. Right now, I need your help with his injured paw—will you help me?"

Colton shifted his weight from foot to foot. He sighed. He looked up at her, and she pleaded with her eyes. She waited, barely breathing. Meg knew she was asking a lot. Colton never lied, and asking him to cover for her was pretty much the same thing. But she also knew that he and his whole family lived for animals, and his conscience wouldn't let him leave one to suffer unnecessarily.

After a minute, he finally spoke. "Yeah, I'll help. Wait here."

He returned a few minutes later with his pockets bulging. "I had to sneak some stuff from the first aid kit, and Mom was trying to get me to watch a movie with her, so it took me a bit. I told her I was going over to your house for birthday cake."

Meg's breath caught in her throat. She hadn't thought about it all day, but she knew there wasn't going to be any birthday cake this year. No one in her house had time to bake one, and buying one was an unnecessary expense. Her parents hadn't had to tell her that—she'd just understood. Embarrassed, she looked away from Colton. "Let's go," she mumbled.

Colton stopped. "You okay?" he asked, his voice soft.

Meg sighed, knowing she'd never be able to hide her feelings from him. "I hadn't even thought about cake," she said. Her eyes were suddenly hot with tears. She willed them not to spill over and run down her cheeks. "I know it's a stupid thing to get upset about, but I just realized that money's too tight for cake." Her voice trembled as she continued. "If we can't afford cake, how on earth are we going to afford a dog? And my parents bought me this really expensive coat for my birthday—I was so selfish to want it in the first place. I should have made my mom return it and get her money back."

"Maybe," Colton replied. "But maybe it's all right for you to have something nice once in a while too. I mean, your parents are the adults. They wouldn't have bought it for you if they couldn't afford to, right? I'm sure they'll figure it all out."

Meg loved that about Colton. He never judged her or anyone else. He was just good and thoughtful and understanding.

"Let's stop by the barn and grab some dog food," he said. "I'll bet this stray of yours is hungry."

Inside the barn, Colton filled a bag with kibble and

grabbed a bowl, a big bottle of water, and a couple of old horse blankets. They packed it all onto a sled they could pull behind them. Loaded down with supplies, they trekked back across the tree farm in comfortable silence.

Even before they reached the shed, Meg could hear Chestnut whining. Her heart pounded as she ran to the door, hoping he was okay. As soon as she opened the latch and swung the splintered wood on its rusty hinges, Chestnut limped toward her, shivering. His eyes were wide and glassy as he surveyed Meg and Colton.

"Oh my gosh," Colton said, his voice filled with concern as he shone his flashlight toward the dog. "He is limping pretty bad, huh?"

They stepped into the shed, and Meg sat down on the ground and patted her knees. Chestnut climbed into her lap and spun around a few times. As the dog nuzzled her eagerly, Colton crouched down and reached out a hand for him to sniff too. Chestnut tore his attention away from Meg to investigate this new person who'd shown up with her. After a moment, Colton stroked Chestnut's side and studied the striped pattern of his fur.

"I think he's a Plott hound," Colton said.

Meg scratched at Chestnut's ears. "A Plott hound? Aren't those pretty expensive dogs?"

"Yeah. They're awesome hunting dogs, and they're excellent trackers."

Colton sat down on the ground beside Meg and continued petting Chestnut. He was gaining the dog's trust before he tried to examine his paw, Meg knew. With his other hand Colton gave Meg the bag of kibble. "Get ready to feed him this while I try to get a good look at his paw, would you?"

Meg scooped out a handful of food, which Chestnut smelled instantly. His whole body wiggled with ravenous excitement. She held her palm out to the dog, who sniffed the kibble for a moment and then gobbled it up nearly in one bite. He was no longer paying any attention to Colton, who gently raised Chestnut's injured white paw and shone his flashlight on it.

Chestnut didn't even seem to notice what Colton

was doing. When all the kibble was gone, he ran his warm tongue across Meg's palm, searching for crumbs. She giggled and held out another handful of food. Chestnut quickly crunched it into bits.

Meanwhile, Colton found the source of Chestnut's wound. "Oh, poor buddy," he said. He drew a pair of tweezers from one of his stuffed pockets.

"What is it?" Meg asked, craning her neck to see while still holding her hand out for Chestnut to eat.

"Hold still, boy," Colton said as he squinted at the paw. "He's got a cut, but there's also a thorn in it. That's probably what's got him limping so bad. It's got to hurt."

Meg held Chestnut still with one hand and kept him furnished with kibble with the other. His fur was smooth and soft against her palm. Colton gripped the dog's injured paw firmly while he carefully removed the thorn with the tweezers. Chestnut jerked his paw and gave a little yelp as Colton worked. Meg's heart jumped to her throat when she felt the dog quiver with fear and pain, but she knew they were helping him. She just wished she could tell him that.

"Shhhhh," she soothed him. "It's okay. I know it hurts right now, but it'll be over in just a sec."

The thorn was out. Colton let his breath out in a rush and ran a hand down Chestnut's neck. "That's going to feel a lot better, buddy. I promise." Colton pulled out a tube of antibiotic ointment and squeezed some onto his fingers before rubbing it into the pad of Chestnut's paw. The dog looked at Meg with fear in his eyes, as though asking her if it was going to hurt anymore. Meg calmed him with a soft stroke and gentle shush. After a few moments, Chestnut returned to his kibble tentatively. Meg felt him lean into her as his body began to relax.

"You should pour him some water," Colton said as he began to wrap the dog's foot in a gauzy bandage. Meg did as she was told. When Colton was finished, Chestnut wiggled to his feet to drink, testing the injured foot gingerly.

Chestnut was thirsty. He lapped at the water without pausing, which gave Colton a chance to check the rest of him over. Colton knelt beside the dog and ran his hands over him lightly, leaning down to look at his belly and the underside of his tail. Meg watched as Colton tugged the burrs out of Chestnut's fur. When he'd had enough water, Chestnut raised his head and stared at Colton for a long moment, as if sizing up the person who was inspecting him—and deciding whether or not he was okay with it. Chestnut must have approved of Colton, because he pushed his cold, wet nose against Colton's hand.

Colton laughed. "It's a real shame," he said, patting Chestnut's side. The dog sat down and rolled over, showing his belly and begging for scratches, which Colton happily provided.

"What is?" Meg asked. Chestnut closed his eyes, stuck all four paws into the air, and let his head loll back, enjoying the attention.

"A beautiful dog like this . . . he must have been abandoned after hunting season. It happens a lot, you know."

"What do you mean?" Meg shuddered at the thought of someone discarding a dog like trash. Especially a sweet, happy pup like Chestnut.

"Hunters breed and train hounds for hunting, but

it costs a lot to take care of them all year long when they're really only 'useful' during hunting season. So after the season is over, some people—not a lot, but some—just take the dogs out into the mountains and leave them."

As if he could understand what Colton was saying, Chestnut wiggled back onto his front, then jumped up on all fours and bounced happily in front of Colton.

"He's thanking you," Meg said.

"You're welcome, pal." Colton smiled, and Chestnut licked his cheek before letting out a happy little grunt and flopping back down on Meg's lap.

She threw her arms around the dog's warm neck. Who would leave an animal alone in the mountains—in the snow and cold? It was the worst thing she'd ever heard, and it broke her heart. She couldn't imagine how confused and sad Chestnut must have been, all alone out there. She looked into his brown eyes, which stared back at her so trustingly. He rested his head on her arm and his lids began to droop. Meg felt like her heart would burst with love for this little guy.

"Well," Colton said, sitting down next to her. "I'm afraid your next move is pretty obvious."

"What do you mean?" Meg asked.

"I mean, I don't think you can keep this poor guy cooped up in this shed. And I don't think you should hide this from your family."

Meg's eyes went wide. Was Colton suggesting that she give up Chestnut? She tried to think of something to say but came up short.

"I've taken care of his paw," he continued. "But he belongs at the shelter, where he can get the care he needs. And a proper home." Colton's eyes were kind as he said the last part, but it still didn't take away the sting Meg felt.

"B-but . . . he found me. He needs me." Chestnut rolled over, so his belly and paws were up. He swatted at Meg's chin while he dozed. "I just have to find a way to convince my mom and dad," she said.

"If he's at the shelter, you can still do that," Colton said. "If your mom and dad come around, maybe you can adopt him."

Meg's mind reeled.

"You need to think strategically, Meg," Colton said. "Promise you'll take him to the shelter first thing in the morning."

The idea of taking Chestnut to a place where she might never see him again made her heart want to shatter into a thousand tiny pieces. But then again, she wasn't sure how long it might take to convince her parents to let her keep him. Maybe Colton's strategy was right. She scratched behind Chestnut's ears. He stirred and looked up at her with big trusting eyes. Maybe the shelter was the best place for him.

Meg took a deep breath. "Promise."

★ CHAPTER 6 ★

Colton spread the horse blankets on the cold ground and called Chestnut over to them. Chestnut stepped onto the fabric and lay right down on them.

"Good boy," Colton singsonged. He picked up the corners of the top blanket and wrapped them around the dog like a canine-size burrito. "There you go." Colton patted Chestnut's head softly and turned to Meg. "I've got to get home," he said. "I promised my mom I'd watch that movie with her when I got back." He pointed to the pile of medical supplies. "I'll leave that stuff here. See that balloon?"

She nodded.

"I clipped off the skinny part of it. Now you can

use the rest to cover his bandage if you take him out on a walk. It'll keep the wound dry. If his bandage gets wet, you'll need to change it."

Meg nodded.

"Colton—" Meg bit her lip, her voice small. "Thanks for your help today. It really means a lot."

He gave her a sad smile. "'Course, Meg the Leg."

Meg smiled back at him, but her heart was heavy with the thought of taking Chestnut to the shelter in the morning. Colton headed for the door, and Chestnut slipped out from under his blanket and trotted over to him, wanting to say goodbye. Colton leaned down and scratched behind the Plott hound's ears for a minute.

"See you, buddy." Colton turned to leave, then looked back over his shoulder at Meg. "Happy birthday again," he said. He hesitated, then went on. "We'll figure something out, about Chestnut. I know we will."

"See you tomorrow," she managed to say through the lump in her throat.

After he left, Meg plopped down onto the blanket. Chestnut trotted over to her and wagged his tail. He had gotten a second wind and looked full of puppy energy.

"You want to walk for a minute before I tuck you in?" Meg asked. Chestnut's ears immediately perked up, and she realized he knew the word *walk*. Someone had to have taught him, which meant that Colton was probably right about him having once belonged to someone.

Meg found the balloon Colton had left behind and stretched it over Chestnut's bandage carefully, making sure it covered all of the gauze. Meg marveled that a regular old party balloon could be a perfect dog boot. She had so much to learn.

"Perfect!" she said, patting Chestnut under the chin. "Let's go."

She grabbed her new purple jacket from the ground, shook it out, and zipped herself in. Then she and Chestnut headed out into the night. The dog walked closely beside her, his head down and his snout hovering over the ground as he sniffed at it with enthusiasm. His gait was thankfully less labored than before. Together, they ducked through the fence, leaving the well-tended rows of trees behind, and entered the woods that surrounded the farm. Meg shone her flashlight on the ground, searching for more perfect pinecones.

This was one of Meg's favorite places on earth. It was so peaceful and silent under the tall trees, with the moonlight reflecting off the snow. The only sound was the soft crunch under her boots and Chestnut's quick breaths as he exhaled sharply to clear his nostrils. Meg inhaled deeply and let the crisp air fill her lungs.

As they wandered through the trees, Meg watched Chestnut closely. There was something different about him—like a change had come over his whole body. His ears were perked up in a new way, and every muscle seemed taut and alert. Almost as if he was *ready* —but for what? They continued exploring, and the more Chestnut sniffed at the ground, the more serious and energized he became. The muscles of his shoulders rippled as he swung his head from side to side rhythmically, methodically.

Meg suddenly realized what he was doing: he was searching for something. Chestnut pressed his nose close to the snow but didn't seem to notice the cold.

He hugged her leg as they walked, as if he was constantly aware of her even as all his senses tuned in to a frequency she couldn't begin to pick up.

Meg was starting to have no doubt that Colton was right. Chestnut wasn't just a happy, goofy stray. He was an expert tracker who'd been abandoned when his usefulness had come to an end.

She got an idea. If Chestnut was a tracking dog, maybe he could help with her project—which would only help her keep him in the end. She stopped walking, and Chestnut froze instantly, one paw still up in the air. He gazed up at her expectantly, like he was waiting for her command. Meg knelt in front of him, holding out one of the pinecones she'd collected. It was time to find out just how good he was at tracking.

He sniffed at the cone excitedly, running his snout up, down, and around it. He even exhaled loudly and sniffed at it again. When he was done, his eyes met hers and she saw that they were bright and alive with anticipation and purpose. Chestnut opened his mouth and let out a near silent bark, snapping his mouth shut. It wasn't an aggressive gesture at all—it was his way of telling her he was ready. She could almost swear he was smiling at her.

"Go on," she said, almost disbelieving. "Go find one."

That was all he needed to hear. Like a shot, Chestnut bolted into the woods, kicking up powdery bursts of snow as he went. His nose down, he plowed a trail across the white ground that Meg could follow. But she didn't. Something told her to wait, and she stayed still, listening to the sound of his paws lightly rising and falling. He was quickly out of sight, but still Meg stayed put. She couldn't even hear him anymore in the silent night.

Meg counted under her breath. *One. Two. Three.* She hadn't made it to four when Chestnut suddenly reappeared through the trees and came bounding back to her, holding something snugly in his mouth. He screeched to a stop right in front of her and dropped a pinecone in the snow at her feet.

"Good boy, Chestnut!" Meg cried. "Can you go find another one?"

He raced off again, gracefully wending around

the trees and through the underbrush as if he'd run through these woods a thousand times. Moments later he returned with another pinecone. Meg praised him and gave him a good solid scratch behind the ears. As soon as he gave her the pinecone, he turned and ran for another.

Back and forth the dog ran, returning over and over again with pinecones that Meg dropped into her backpack until it was weighted down with them. When she couldn't fit another cone into her bag and Chestnut was panting from exertion, she held out her hands, palm up. "That's it," she said. "We're all done."

Immediately, he sat in front of her, his ears perked for her next instruction.

"Come on, buddy," she said, petting him. Meg was relieved to discover that Chestnut wasn't just a little trained—he was *well* trained. That would make convincing her parents that much easier. She hefted the heavy backpack onto her shoulders and adjusted its bulk on her back.

"Let's get you back to the shed, boy," she said, looking up to see that the moon had gotten higher overhead. It was late—she really needed to get back. Meg moved swiftly, and Chestnut mirrored her gait with little effort. They made their way through the forest side by side, like old friends.

Back at the shed, Meg peeled the protective balloon off the dog's paw. His bandage had stayed nice and dry. She poured more water into his dish and fed him some more kibble, which he gobbled eagerly from her hand. Then she sat down on the horse blankets Colton had brought and patted the ground beside her. "Time to sleep, Chestnut," she said. Chestnut stepped onto the blanket and pawed at it, bunching it up in front of him. He spun around a few times before flopping down next to her, his tongue lolling out of his mouth as he panted. "You worked hard, didn't you, boy?"

He snuggled into the blanket, looking tuckered out from their adventure. Meg stayed put for a long moment, running her fingers along the brindled stripes on his side. "That's a good boy, Chestnut. You're a good boy."

As Chestnut started to breathe more slowly, Meg

stood up. "I'll be back in the morning," she said, crouching down for one last pet. She pulled a corner of the blanket over him and kissed the top of his head. "I promise." He looked at her with sad eyes but didn't move to follow.

Meg closed and latched the shed door behind her. She desperately wanted to stay with Chestnut, but she had no time to waste. Because Meg had just decided something. She wasn't going to take Chestnut to the shelter. If she lost him forever, she would never forgive herself. She just had to prove that she could keep him, before her parents or Colton found out.

Meg hurried away from the shed without looking back. She was eager to put her plan into action.

She needed to get home. There was work to do.

★ CHAPTER 7 ★

As soon as she returned home and removed her winter layers, Meg went into the kitchen. Her family was finishing up dinner, but Meg didn't join them at the table. She was single-minded as she filled her mom's cookie sheets with pinecones. She put them in the oven on low heat, hoping to bake out any bugs that might be hiding within them. This would also dry out the dampness that had settled into the ones that had been buried under the snow. While she waited for them to bake, she stood by the sink and scarfed down a huge portion of her dad's famous spaghetti. Then she helped clean up the dinner dishes, distracted the whole time by thoughts of the adventures she and Chestnut could have together.

"What's all this stuff for?" Ben asked, pointing at the oven when Meg opened it to peek at the pinecones.

"It's a craft project," she replied. "I'm going to make some ornaments to sell at the tree lot." This time she didn't feel shy about saying it out loud. She announced her plan like it was a known fact.

Ben grinned at her. "You do love to craft, don't you, Micro?"

Meg was too focused on her work to notice that he'd used her nickname again. She nodded but kept her eyes trained on the roasting pinecones through the window on the oven door.

Sarah stood up, still looking at her phone, and announced, "I'm going over to Jenna's house. That okay, Mom?" Jenna was Sarah's best friend, and she lived in town with her grandparents.

Meg's mom nodded distractedly at Sarah. "That's fine for a little while."

Ben yawned loudly, pushing himself up to standing

as well. "I'm going to take a hot shower and pass out watching YouTube."

Their mom shot Ben a pointed look. "Don't use all the hot water, Ben," she said. "I've got sap in my hair that's going to take forever to get out."

As Sarah pulled on her boots, their dad called out from across the kitchen. He had his head buried in the fridge, where he was trying to squeeze in the leftovers. "Home by ten, Sarah-Bear. Tomorrow's going to be crazy."

Sarah grabbed the truck keys from the hook. "'Kay, Dad. Hope you had a good birthday, kiddo," she said, ruffling Meg's hair on her way past. "See you in the morning."

After Sarah shut the door behind her and Ben clomped noisily up the stairs, Meg pulled the trays of pinecones from the oven. When they were cool, she piled them all into a big bowl, then turned to her parents. "I'm going up to my room to work on these. I want to get a good start before bed."

Her mom nodded, but her dad put on an exaggerated pout. "You don't want to watch a little TV with your old man?"

Upstairs, the shower turned on and Ben's voice rang out, singing the theme song from a silly kids' cartoon at the top of his lungs.

"Sorry," she said with a shrug. "I really want to get going on these ornaments. Rain check?"

Her parents exchanged a surprised look. "Of course, sweetie. Don't stay up too late."

Her mom glanced at the pinecones again and her face softened. She pulled Meg into a hug. "Happy birthday," she said into her hair. "I'm sorry it was such a quiet one."

Meg looked up into her mother's eyes. "No, Mom —don't say that! It was perfect." Meg realized that she meant it. It *had* been a quiet birthday, but it had also been her best one ever. She just couldn't tell her mom that—not yet.

Then she gathered her bowl of pinecones and headed upstairs to her room before her mom could say anything more.

In Meg's room, her art table was laden with paints and brushes, glitter, glue, beads, ribbons, and rhinestones. There was even the pretty paper from her birthday present, folded neatly, just waiting to be turned into something beautiful.

Once Meg was seated at her table, the pinecones spread out before her in a seemingly endless array, she began to feel a little overwhelmed. There were so many. And her head was so full of ideas that she didn't know where to start. But staring at them wasn't getting her any closer to making money to help the farm —or to keeping Chestnut.

She smiled to herself, remembering the dog's silly antics. He was such a sweet boy, so full of excitement and purpose. Just thinking about Chestnut made her heart swell. It seemed impossible because she'd just found him that morning, but she was already so crazy about him.

Meg stared down at the pinecone in front of her and an idea sprang to life. She closed her eyes for a second, letting the picture fill itself in. That was it!

Her eyes popped open, and she grabbed a bottle

of brown paint and another of black. She poured the black into a little dish and dipped the narrow pinecone into it, slowly rotating it to make sure it was evenly coated. Then she poured the brown into a separate dish and mixed it with a little red, giving it more of a vibrant hue. She could picture Chestnut's velvety, rich fur and she wanted to match the color perfectly.

While the black was drying, she dug through her beads, looking for the perfect ones to be his eyes. Finally, she found what she was looking for—two identical black teardrop-shaped glass beads—the size a perfect match. Meg took out a fine-tipped brush, dipped it into the reddish-brown, and carefully painted Chestnut's telltale brindle stripes. Then she used her hot glue gun to attach the beads to the pinecone body. They glittered like the dog's real eyes had when he was on the hunt for this very pinecone.

She couldn't help but grin as the miniature Chestnut came to life in her hands. She hot-glued little ears and a tail made of felt to his body, then small sticks for legs. For the finishing touch, she added a pink felt tongue that made him look like he was panting with excitement. Looking down at his handmade replica, she could picture Chestnut in her mind. She felt his slobbery kisses and soft fur. The thought of him made her feel happy — and hopeful.

She was done. Meg held out the pinecone to admire her work. It was the perfect ornament for the perfect dog, and she would do whatever it took to make sure that he was hers, forever. Meg put the ornament to the side to dry. This ornament — this silly dog that looked like her Chestnut — wasn't for sale. This little guy was her birthday gift to herself.

The thing that Meg had always loved most about crafting was taking something simple, or even useless, and turning it into something new, beautiful, and meaningful. It had been easy to know what to make for herself, but what would other people want for their trees?

She picked up one of the pinecones and turned it this way and that, admiring the way it almost looked like a miniature Fraser fir. She closed her eyes, remembering how the trees had looked that morning when she had left the house. Set against the sunny winter sky, their needles were bright green, and there was a dusting of glittering snow atop their branches. The trees had looked like wintry magic. Maybe the tree lot customers would be as inspired by them as she was.

Meg picked up bottles of green and white paint and poured out some of each color. She thought it might be possible to give the pinecones the same sort of effect that the wintry firs had, but she couldn't just dump a bunch of glitter onto a sticky pinecone, like a kindergartner would. No, she needed to paint them the perfect green, then layer on the white snow and sparkling ice crystals with a delicate hand.

With the vision in her head, she got to work.

Meg was so focused that she lost track of time. "Don't stay up too much longer, Meggie," her mom said from the doorway. "Morning will be here before you know it."

"I won't. I just have a little more to do," Meg answered distractedly.

Meg didn't know how long she dipped and sprinkled, glued and tweezered, but eventually her desk was laden with unique creations. She paused to stretch her arms over her head and looked carefully at her work. The pinecones had been transformed into something else entirely—something more than a little arts-and-crafts project. Each one was a bit of winter beauty that would last all year.

By the time she finished all the pinecones, Meg's eyes were heavy and her arms were stiff, but she knew she couldn't quit yet. She needed to add a ribbon to each and every ornament so customers could hang them from their trees.

Meg got out a ball of twine and several rolls of ribbon. She dropped a bead of hot glue at the top of each pinecone and held a short piece of ribbon or twine to it until it dried. Then she knotted the ends of each strand together tightly.

As she attached the last bit of twine to the last tree, her vision was getting blurry and her head had begun to pound with exhaustion. At last, there was only one ornament left—her miniature Chestnut ornament. She snipped off a stretch of beautiful purple ribbon. It was her favorite color, and it was for her favorite dog. Meg's fingers ached from the hours of delicate work as she attached it. But she was finally finished. Now she could rest.

Meg glanced at her watch and her heart sank. It was nearly morning—she had worked through the entire night. She could barely keep her eyes open. How would she get through the day?

She changed quickly into her pajamas and collapsed into bed, reminding herself that she had done this for the farm and for Chestnut.

Chestnut.

Was he all right, all alone? But Meg had no time to worry before her eyelids began to droop heavily and she fell, finally, to sleep.

★ CHAPTER 8 ★

Meg was running with Chestnut through the woods. The dog hurtled over rocks and tree branches with ease, and Meg kept up with little effort. Snow fell lightly on her cheeks. Suddenly Ben's voice echoed in the air all around her, and a warm light crossed her face. It was so loud and bright . . . what was happening?

"*Micro!*" Ben boomed. Meg's eyes popped open, and for a second she was confused. Her head slowly began to clear, and she rubbed her eyes and looked around her room. Morning sunlight streamed through the window onto her bed, and Ben yelled to her through her door.

"Hey, Micro. Daylight's wasting!" He rapped

sharply with his knuckles. "You're going to miss break-fast if you don't get a move on."

Groaning, Meg dragged herself out of bed and into her clothes. She was only half aware of eating her breakfast or brushing her hair and teeth. At the last minute, she remembered that she needed to pack up her ornaments to take to the tree lot. Nervously, she touched the edge of one of them, testing to see if they'd had enough time to dry. She let out an exhale of relief when the glue and paint were smooth and dry to the touch.

Meg gathered up her ornaments, quickly but gently placing them into a cute basket. If her plan was going to work, she needed things to go smoothly today. She tucked the last painted pinecone tree into its spot and stepped back to look at it. The finished project filled her with renewed excitement.

She looked at the clock. She'd have to *run* to the shed if she wanted to check on Chestnut and still make it to the lot on time. She grabbed her coat, mittens, and basket, and shook herself awake. She needed to be on her game today.

After giving Chestnut a few scratches and some kibble and water, Meg raced to the tree lot, where she placed the basket next to the cash register with a sign that said HANDMADE FRASER FIR ORNAMENTS — $5.00. She was still out of breath as she wiped away the beads of sweat on her forehead under her warm hat. Immediately, her stomach began to twist with nerves. What if customers didn't like her creations? What if she didn't sell a single one?

In the morning light, the glitter and beads sparkled like ice crystals, just as she'd wanted them to. Any hope she had of keeping Chestnut was riding on these ornaments. But what if people thought they looked silly and childish?

There wasn't much time to worry about that, because her dad was right. The sunshine had brought the customers out in droves, and the day was even busier than the one before. Meg's whole family and the entire staff were rushing around helping people. There was such a steady stream of customers at the register that she had to use all her focus to make sure she was counting correctly and not forgetting what change she owed customers.

"Wow, honey!" a man's voice broke through the holiday music and bubbly chatter all around. "Look at these ornaments. Don't they look just like the sun hitting the snow on a tree? First thing in the morning when we're out walking the dog?"

Meg's heart pounded in her chest as the man's wife stepped over to examine her artwork.

"Yes!" the woman replied, her eyes getting big and round. She picked out a couple of pinecones. "Aren't they just beautiful? They'll look perfect on the tree. We'll take these two," she said, holding them out to Meg at her register. "Along with the tree over there, and the wreath."

Meg beamed. "I'm so glad you like them," she said to the woman as she rang up the sale.

"Are you the artist who makes them?" the man said, handing her the money.

Meg felt her cheeks go red. "I . . . Yes, I mean, I made the ornaments."

"You're very talented," the woman said, dangling

the decorated pinecones from her finger. "I just love them!"

"Thank you," Meg said, grinning broadly.

The couple turned to walk away, and Meg called after them. "We'll see you back here at Briggs Family Tree Farm next year!" She was supposed to say that to every customer, but she was so tired and overwhelmed that she almost forgot.

Late in the morning, Meg looked up and saw that the next person in line wasn't a customer at all.

It was Colton.

"Colton, how are you?" Meg's mom asked as she held out her hand for a woman's credit card. Her mom had always liked Colton. At first Meg had thought it was because he was Meg's first best friend, but over time she developed a sneaking suspicion that it was really because he complimented her mom's cooking. A lot.

"Good morning, Mrs. Briggs," Colton said, polite as always. "Hey, Meg."

"What's up?" Meg asked, trying to act naturally.

She pulled her apron straight and brushed off loose tree needles from her coat sleeves.

"Got a minute?" Colton asked Meg, eyeing her mom.

Meg's heart pounded in her chest. Something in Colton's voice made her squirmy.

Meg quickly glanced over his shoulder, making sure there wasn't a line at her register. Luckily there was a lull in the action.

"Hey, Mom?" Meg asked. "Can I take a quick break?" She tried to sound nonchalant.

Her mom glanced around the tree lot. "Five minutes," she said, as another car full of customers pulled up and parked. "And then check the cocoa and cookies."

"Thanks." Meg made sure her register was locked, then glanced over her shoulder at Colton. "Come on," she said, hoping that her mom couldn't sense her nervousness. They went into the stock trailer and Meg double-checked to make sure they were alone.

"What's up?" she asked, trying not to sound like she was hiding something from her best friend.

Colton sighed, leaning against one of the stacks of boxes. "I just wanted to see how it went at the shelter this morning."

Meg chewed on her bottom lip. She had to tell Colton something that would sound like the truth without *actually* telling him the truth. Heat rushed to her cheeks. She'd never lied to him before, but she wasn't ready to give up Chestnut.

"Good," she said, turning her back to Colton and rearranging some receipt paper on the shelves.

Colton exhaled. "I know that must've been hard," he said. "I'm sorry I couldn't go with you. I had a chess tournament."

"It's okay," Meg said, still not turning around. "Did you win?"

Her best friend shook his head and began helping her restack the rolls of paper.

"Look, Meg. I'm not sure if now is the time to say this, but—" Colton searched for the right words. "I really think you did the right thing. For you *and* Chestnut."

Meg sighed. It suddenly felt like the weight of the world was on her shoulders. She hated lying to her friend. The guilt twisted inside her. But she also hated the idea that Chestnut was scared and unhappy in the shed while she was working and couldn't go see him. And to make matters worse, now she couldn't ask for Colton's help. Meg was totally on her own, and she didn't know much about taking care of dogs. She buried her face in her hands.

Colton put his hand on her shoulder. "It'll be okay," he said, his trademark grin back in place. "It might take some time, but everything will work out in the end. Chestnut's going to be okay, got it?" Colton held up his fist, and Meg bumped it.

She just hoped he was right.

Time passed in a blur as Meg helped a steady stream of customers. She sold trees and wreaths, garlands and goodies, but by noon, she still hadn't sold a single ornament since the first couple had come by.

Meg was starting to get nervous. She didn't have a

plan B. If no one else liked her ornaments, how would she ever be able to convince her parents to keep her new dog—let alone a dog who was anxious and needed a *lot* of time, love, and attention?

Meg began to feel a sinking sense of dread. A question that had been nagging at her, way deep down, was worming its way to the top of her mind: What if this didn't work out?

★ CHAPTER 9 ★

As the day progressed, Meg's lack of sleep finally started to catch up to her. Once, during a lull between customers, she snuck into the storage trailer, leaned against a pile of boxes, and let her heavy eyelids close.

"You all right, sis?" Sarah asked as she stepped into the trailer, letting the door slam shut behind her. "You look exhausted."

Meg startled and blinked. "Yep," she said, forcing herself to sound cheerful. "It's just been a busy day."

A big yawn escaped Meg's lips, and Sarah arched an eyebrow at her. "It has been a busy day. But not so busy that you should be falling asleep standing up. What's going on?"

For a heartbeat, Meg considered telling her sister everything. Telling her about Chestnut, about all of her work to prove that she could take care of him, about how she'd lied to Colton. But something stopped her. What if Sarah laughed at her? What if Sarah said that she was too young and silly to save Chestnut? What if she agreed that the shelter was the best place for him?

Instead, Meg let out a laugh that sounded false to her ears, but she hoped Sarah didn't notice. "I don't know . . . I'm just tired, I guess. Nothing worth talking about."

Sarah shrugged and grabbed a cookie off a sheet pan resting nearby. "You want one?" she asked, passing the wreath-shaped sweet with red and green sprinkles to Meg.

"Thanks," Meg said. "How's your day going?"

Sarah picked up her own cookie—a triangular tree coated in green frosting—and took a bite. "I'm great," she said through a mouthful. "Business is good, Christmas is almost here, and I should be hearing from NC State any day now."

"It's going to be weird if you go away to college," Meg said, her voice a little raspy.

Sarah had a faraway look on her face. "Change is always scary, but it's not like I'm going to disappear forever. I'll only be an hour away. And I'll be home all summer and definitely for the Christmas rush."

Meg was suddenly filled with an inexplicable sadness. She tried to imagine what it would be like with one less person in the house—especially if that person was Sarah. Meg would spend less time waiting for the bathroom, but also less time laughing, shopping at the mall, or talking to her big sister. She hadn't been worried about Sarah leaving for college, and yet . . . her heart felt even heavier. Here was another thing to pile on top of everything else.

It must have shown on her face, because Sarah grabbed her by the shoulder and pulled her into a hug. "Don't worry, Meggie," she said with a laugh. "I haven't even gotten in yet."

"I know," Meg said. "I'm excited for you. Don't worry about me."

Sarah grabbed another cookie. "One for the road," she said. "You coming?"

Meg nodded. "I'll be out in a minute," she said, nibbling on her cookie.

Sarah grabbed an armful of Styrofoam cups and left the storage shed. When she was gone, Meg collapsed against the boxes with a sigh. Rather than easing her mind, her conversation with Sarah had just made her more anxious. Everything in her life felt complicated. What if nothing worked out and everything was worse than it was before? She wished she could tell her sister what was going on.

Meg was overcome by a deep, wide yawn. She shook off her sleepiness, crunched the last of her snack, and left the trailer—and hopefully her worries—behind.

But as the day wore on, her fears only intensified. After the initial interest in her ornaments, not a single customer purchased one. By the afternoon, Meg's heart was as heavy as her eyelids. The ornaments weren't going to help save Chestnut, and Meg had wasted an entire night for nothing.

She stumbled through the rest of the day. Every

time she glanced at Sarah, her sister was watching her with concern. Meg knew that her sister suspected something was up. What was she going to tell her to keep her from getting curious?

Just as they were getting ready to close up the tree lot, a woman approached the register. "Hi there," she said, smiling brightly. "I understand that you're the artist behind these beautiful ornaments." She nodded toward Sarah, who was talking quietly with their mom. "Your sister told me that you make these all yourself." Sarah and their mom looked over at Meg, and Meg's heart pounded a little harder. She hoped they didn't know how late she'd stayed up.

"Yes, ma'am," Meg answered the woman with a smile of her own. She tried to push away her thoughts about Sarah.

"Where do you get all the pinecones? Are they all local?" the woman asked.

"They are," Meg replied. "Every single one is from right here on Briggs Family Tree Farm."

The woman's eyes lit up. "That's wonderful!" She waved her hands excitedly at the trees and wreaths nearby. "My friends and I are in charge of decorating the Christmas tree at city hall this year. The theme is a Carolina Christmas, and I'm going to ask them to come here, to see if they agree. But I think your ornaments really represent what's best about North Carolina and the heritage of the Fraser fir. I hope you have a lot more!" The woman's singsong voice rang out.

"Oh—wow!" For a second Meg didn't know what to say. "Um—how many more would you need?"

"Well, we'd need a few hundred at least," the woman said. She saw the shocked look on Meg's face. "It's a really big tree!" she added by way of explanation.

Meg gulped but tried to seem calm. "That's no problem! I can make that happen."

The woman sized Meg up and nodded knowingly. "You really are quite the artist. I'm going to buy a few of these for my own tree before you sell out."

She spent a few moments poking through the ornaments, a few oohs and aahs escaping her mouth. She finally picked four and paid for them.

"Thank you so much," Meg said.

"Thank you, darlin'." The woman turned to leave.

"I'll be back with the planning committee to have them take a look. Just imagine, your ornaments representing Christmas for the whole city . . ."

Meg could barely breathe. If she sold a bunch of ornaments to this lady and her friends, it might just solve all of her problems! Then again, this woman had said she needed a few *hundred*. Meg had no idea how she was going to make hundreds of ornaments in time. But she'd just have to figure it out.

She felt a sudden burst of adrenaline. She finished shutting down the register and helped put away the wreaths, garlands, and refreshments. Her heart was skipping with excitement as the last customer's minivan pulled out of the lot with a tree tied to the top, and she helped her family close up for the night.

Meg was willing to give up any amount of sleep for Chestnut. And if this worked out with the city hall tree, she'd sell enough ornaments to keep her dog. For the first time all day, things were starting to look up.

★ CHAPTER 10 ★

The tree lot was finally dark and quiet, and Meg couldn't wait to spend time with Chestnut. Even though she was tired, having a pet meant that she had to be responsible for him, no matter what. And most of all, she knew that Chestnut needed to get out of that small space and use up some energy. Every time she'd thought about him, all afternoon, it was almost as if she could hear him whining and scratching to get out the door. She knew he must be going crazy in there.

Meg's dad locked the gate and rubbed his eyes with both hands. Her mom yawned deeply. Meg looked from one to the other and cleared her throat.

"I'm going to go hang out with Colton for a bit before dinner, if that's okay," Meg said.

Her dad just nodded, but her mom eyed her a little strangely.

"Don't you think you ought to be getting some rest tonight?" her mom said. "You look awfully worn out."

Meg grinned to cover her exhaustion. "I'm fine!" she said, cheerfully. "I won't be gone too long, but I wanted to tell him about the ornaments—how that woman might want so many of them."

"Okay," her mom said, straightening Meg's ponytail. "But don't be too late. We're having hamburgers for dinner."

"I won't, Mom. I promise."

Meg waited until they'd driven away, then ran toward the shed, bursting with excitement to see Chestnut again.

When she opened the creaky door, an eager, hyper dog rushed toward her.

"Hi, buddy!"

Meg sat down to greet him, and he bathed her face in so many dog kisses she had to squeeze her eyes and mouth shut to dodge his tongue. Chestnut was so happy to see her that he only stopped long enough to run laps around the shed, zooming in circles before coming back for more kisses.

Meg laughed out loud as she watched him go, amazed that she already loved him so much. After a few minutes, Chestnut finally slowed down and plopped onto the ground at her knee. He rolled over, panting hard, and she stroked his belly while he laid his head on her lap. He seemed so content—just as Meg was.

As she scratched him, Meg scanned the shed, and what she saw made her suck in her breath. It was clear that Chestnut had not been happy to be left alone for the day. There were scratch marks all over the wood walls and doorframe. One of the horse blankets had been chewed nearly in half, its edges frayed and full of holes. The rest were scattered around the space like they'd been dragged and stomped on.

Her heart broke a little bit. She looked down at the sweet creature who was clearly so content now, just being with her. It was hard to believe he'd been so miserable that he did all that damage, but he had. If only she'd been there, he wouldn't have had to feel like that.

"Did you miss me, buddy?" she asked. Chestnut cocked his head and locked eyes with her in response, his eyebrows bunched together and his tongue lolling from the side of his mouth. He pawed her hand to remind her to keep scratching his belly.

Meg giggled.

But before she could pet him again, Chestnut rolled over, hopped to his feet, and perked his head toward the door. In the same instant, Meg heard the door creak behind her. Someone else was there. Meg's heart pounded as she turned around slowly to see who it was.

It was Colton. And he didn't look happy.

"I thought I might find you here," Colton said.

"I'm so sorry, Colton," Meg blurted out. "I wanted to tell you. I really did."

Colton's expression remained stony as he slowly leaned his bike against the wall of the shed.

"I went over to your house to hang out," he said evenly. "But they said you were at *my* house . . . so then I figured out what was up. Guess you didn't take Chestnut to the shelter after all."

"Well, I was going to. And then I came up with a plan to sell ornaments at the farm so that we could afford to keep him, and then I was afraid that you'd be mad at me, so I didn't tell you the truth earlier. I felt awful about it and wanted to tell you everything." Meg was talking a mile a minute, but she couldn't seem to stop herself. "I never want to lie to you ever again, Colton. I mean it."

Meg searched Colton's eyes, hoping that he believed her. Instead, he just looked around the shed. "Oh boy, Chestnut doesn't like being alone, huh?" Meg waited for him to say something else, which felt like it took forever. "Hmm," was all he said after a few moments.

"Could you, um, maybe share what you're *hmm*ing about?" Meg asked anxiously.

Several more seconds passed.

"It's pretty common for a dog like Chestnut to have some separation anxiety." He looked at the chewed horse blanket and something flickered in his eyes. "And from this . . . situation . . . it seems pretty likely."

Meg bristled at Colton's tone. He made it sound like Chestnut had some sort of problem. She looked away and poured the dog some more kibble. "Well, I don't plan on being separated from him for long," she said. "That will go away when he can live with me and we can be together all the time."

Colton eyed her skeptically. "It's not always that easy," he said, his tone softening. "Sometimes you have to work really hard to train a dog out of being afraid."

"Would you like being cooped up all day?" Meg snapped, unable to keep the frustration out of her voice.

Colton held out a hand, palm first, to make peace. "It's okay, Meg. I get it—I'm not trying to tell you he's a bad dog."

She took a breath and reminded herself that this wasn't Colton's fault. He was just trying to help. "Sorry." She closed her eyes and waited until her emotions calmed down. "All I'm saying is that I'm sure Chestnut is fine," she said.

Colton shrugged, letting it go, and grabbed the first aid kit. "Come here, boy," he said, clucking his tongue at Chestnut. With Meg there, Chestnut was totally comfortable with him. The dog trotted over and sat down next to Colton, then held up his injured paw to be examined. Colton removed the bandage and looked closely at the wound. "It's healing up really well," he said. He applied some more salve and wrapped Chestnut's foot in a new bandage, then held out his nose for a kiss, which Chestnut happily provided.

Chestnut jumped up and pranced around the inside of the shed, zigzagging and bobbing his head in a happy dance. Then he ran back to them, his whole rump swaying as he wagged his tail in wide swoops. He gave Colton one more lick on the nose, then dropped to the ground. He rolled over onto his back and jabbed his paws in the air, ready for another belly rub. Meg grinned, scratching the dog's belly.

Wiping his face on his sleeve, Colton laughed at the dog's antics. "I think he's good as new."

"Let's get him outside," Meg said. She was, as always, so grateful for her friend's good nature.

They set off into the surrounding woods, Chestnut walking between them. The Plott hound looked up at Meg, and she could have sworn he was smiling again.

"I'm happy to be out with you, too," she said, patting Chestnut on the head.

As they walked, Chestnut's whole demeanor transformed, as it had the night before. He stepped out ahead of them, and his head dropped and hovered over the ground. His muscles flexed and his tail went up.

"Look at that," Colton said, eyeing the dog thoughtfully. "He's tracking."

"That's what happened last night, too," Meg said. "And you won't believe what he did next." She pulled a pinecone from her jacket pocket and called to the dog. He snapped back to her side. When she stopped walking, he did too. She held out the pinecone for Chestnut to sniff. When the dog was done, he watched Meg carefully, waiting for her command.

"Chestnut, go find it!" Meg said. The pup shot off through the trees and disappeared from view.

Colton's mouth hung open, and Meg laughed at her friend's surprised expression.

"He's kind of awesome, right?" she said.

"Kind of?" Colton shook his head. "He's amazing."

"I think you were right about one thing, Colt

—somebody abandoned Chestnut. He knows how to do so many things. And the fact that he can find these pinecones is huge." Meg told Colton about the lady who wanted hundreds of ornaments. "If that order really happens, Chestnut is my only shot at getting it done."

Colton nodded, and a smile spread across his face. "I mean, it must have been awful for Chestnut to be dumped outside and left to fend for himself. But it's really cool that you found him." Colton looked at Meg, and for the first time, she saw in his face that he understood how she felt about Chestnut. "He's got some skills, Meg. That'll make it easier to get your mom and dad to let you keep him. If he's trained, I mean."

Just then, Chestnut came bounding out of the woods toward them. He stopped at their feet with a pinecone tucked snugly in his mouth. "Drop it," Colton said, pointing at the ground. Chestnut gently laid it on the ground, and Colton bent to pick it up. He studied the pinecone in his hand as if it held a clue to the mystery of Chestnut's life. He looked at the panting dog, who was patiently waiting for praise, a treat, or his next command. Colton gave him all three.

"He's a really good dog, Meg," he said, as Chestnut scrambled back into the woods in search of the next pinecone.

"I know he is," Meg said proudly.

They were quiet as they waited for Chestnut to return. When he dropped a new pinecone at their feet, she scratched him behind the ears. "Who's a good dog? Huh?" she asked, pursing her lips at him. "Is Chestnut a good dog?"

Chestnut thumped his tail on the ground in agreement and let out a happy snort. Meg and Colton laughed.

When Chestnut had cleared their immediate area of loose pinecones, he tromped farther through the trees in search of his quarry. While he was gone, Meg wandered a few yards away to sit on a tree stump. A few moments later, Chestnut returned with his most recent discovery, but when he spotted Colton—and not Meg—he froze. He dropped the pinecone and let out a sharp and frightened bark.

"What is it?" Colton asked. Chestnut whimpered in response, then spun around in a circle, anxiously scanning the area until he spotted Meg. He raced over to her and stood up on his hind legs, pawing at her and whimpering.

"Chestnut!" Meg said, alarmed. "What's the matter?" She wrapped her arms around him and tried to soothe the shaking dog. Meg looked up at Colton, who had a strange look on his face. "Do you think he—" She didn't even want to finish the question, because she already knew the answer.

Colton nodded, his mouth pressed into a grim line. "Yeah. He was upset because he didn't see you right away. He thought you were gone."

They were quiet for a moment, both thinking about what that meant. Chestnut, reassured that Meg wasn't going anywhere, sat down in front of her and waited for his next command. Meg held out the pinecone in her pocket and told him to find another one. The dog took off into the woods.

Meg watched him go, then felt Colton's eyes on her. She turned to him, and the friends shared a knowing look. They didn't have to tell each other how they felt, because they both understood. Chestnut needed help.

Meg forced herself to smile. "It just means that we've already bonded," she said, her tone sounding more optimistic than she felt.

"You definitely have," Colton said, trying to be supportive. "But he was really anxious. That's not good, Meg. I mean, what happens when you have to go to school? Is he going to tear apart your house looking for you?"

Meg looked at the ground. She didn't know the answer. "Maybe he just needs time," she said, though she wasn't sure if she was trying to convince Colton or herself of that. "He's been through a lot and he still manages to be the sweetest dog I've ever met. He'll be okay." She locked eyes with Colton again. "He has to be okay, Colt."

She ignored the doubtful expression on her best friend's face. She was too tired to worry about that just now.

Chestnut returned, and they continued to send him out on pinecone missions. After a while, the dog seemed to get bored with the game.

"Let's change it up a little." Colton walked a

hundred feet or so into the woods, where he was out of sight. When he came back, Meg noticed that he wasn't wearing his coat. He had hidden it behind a tree.

"Aren't you cold?" She laughed.

Colton shivered. "Yup. So he'd better find it fast." He held out his hand for Chestnut to sniff. "Go find it!" Colton commanded, and the dog was gone in an instant.

Meg immediately started counting. "One-Mississippi, two-Mississippi . . ."

Exactly twenty-seven Mississippis later, Chestnut bounded back to them, dragging Colton's jacket —which was now covered in leaves and dirt—on the ground.

"Nice!" Colton said, grabbing the coat and putting it on without even brushing it off. "I wasn't going to make it much longer, so thanks for doing that so fast, man." He gave Chestnut a treat and scratched him under the chin.

"Under thirty seconds!" Meg pulled off her new purple jacket. "I want to try."

"That was way too easy. Make it harder for him," Colton said. "See if you can make it take a full minute."

Meg looked around, deciding which direction would be best. She loved the idea of challenging Chestnut, and she thought it would be an opportunity to prove Colton wrong about the dog's anxiety, too. She knew Chestnut was a good boy. He'd never be destructive just because he was worried about her being gone. "Okay," she said, grinning. "Keep him busy for a minute so he doesn't miss me."

She slipped between the trees and tiptoed down into a narrow creek bed. She jumped over the snowy dip in the center and found a fallen log on the other bank. She hopped over it and saw that it was partly hollow on the far side. *Perfect*. Meg tucked her new coat into the shell of the tree, then turned and ran back to the clearing, where Colton was wrestling with Chestnut. Colton was laughing, and the dog barked happily.

When Chestnut saw Meg, he broke away from Colton and trotted over to her playfully.

"Let's time this one the official way." Colton pulled

out his phone and held his thumb over the timer. He nodded at Meg that he was ready. She held her hand under Chestnut's nose. He immediately calmed down, sat attentively, and sniffed at her knuckles. "Go find it, boy," she said, pointing toward the trees so he knew to go.

Chestnut hurried off, his nose pressed to the ground as he followed her scent. Colton started the timer.

"This time it'll be hard — it's going to take him a little bit." She looked sideways at her friend. Colton was watching the trees where Chestnut had disappeared. "And when he comes back and doesn't see me, he's going to be totally fine — watch."

Colton's head snapped around to look at her. "Are you going to —"

Meg didn't wait for him to finish the sentence. She snuck off into the woods, in the opposite direction from Chestnut, and ducked behind a large snow-covered tree stump. She waited, peering around the side so she could watch what Chestnut would do.

After a moment, Chestnut returned with her coat in his mouth, galloping cheerfully back to Colton. But when the dog saw that Meg wasn't there, he began to panic. His eyes grew wide and he swung his head from side to side, looking for her.

"Go find Meg, boy," Colton said. "Go on!"

Chestnut still gripped her coat by the sleeve. As the dog scurried around searching for Meg, the coat dragged along the snowy, uneven ground. Even from where she hid, Meg could hear a low growl forming in the back of Chestnut's throat. A little feeling of guilt began to gnaw at her. She hated seeing him this upset. The longer it took for Chestnut to find her, the more and more anxious he grew. Meg's heart pounded in her chest as she watched him begin to shake with stress.

She couldn't deny it any longer. Colton was right. When Meg was out of his sight, Chestnut transformed into a different dog—a panicked creature that had once been abandoned and lived in fear that it would happen again. She couldn't bear to watch him suffer any longer.

Just as Meg was about to stand up and call him over, Chestnut turned in her direction. His nose twitched, his ears went up, and his eyes locked on the snowy mound that hid her from view. As he took off in her direction, the coat snagged on a low branch. In his desperation to get to Meg, Chestnut yanked hard on the coat. It broke loose, and a second later he screeched to a halt at Meg's side, dropped the coat on the ground, and—his tail tucked between his legs—whimpered and whined and climbed right into her lap. He was panting from exertion and fear.

"Oh, Chestnut, I'm sorry." Meg fought a lump in her throat. No one had ever needed her like this before, and it was a little overwhelming. "You're such a good boy." She held his face in both hands and looked into his sad eyes. She ran her thumbs along his face and kissed him on the snout, then gave him a couple soft pats on the side to show him she was happy to see him.

Chestnut raised one paw and placed it firmly over her arm, as if to say she had to stay right where she was. For good.

Meg shivered in the cold. She reached out her free arm to grab her coat from the ground. When she went to ease her arm through the sleeve, she gasped in horror.

There was a gaping hole right through the sleeve of her new, expensive coat.

Tears sprang to her eyes and rolled down her cheeks. Meg began to panic. What would she tell her parents? She could never hide this from them — her mom would notice the damage right away.

Meg freed her other arm from under Chestnut's paw and buried her face in her hands. Why couldn't she do anything right anymore?

Meg was breathing in a fast, shallow rhythm. She forced herself to breathe slowly and deeply to try to calm herself. But nothing could chase away the thought that was playing on repeat in her head: not only was her new coat destroyed, but she also had to get home and prepare to make hundreds more ornaments. A wave of exhaustion suddenly washed over her.

Being responsible was a lot harder than she'd expected.

★ CHAPTER 11 ★

When Meg arrived home everyone was busy in the kitchen, putting the final touches on dinner. Her dad stood at the stove, wearing his silly "Kiss the Cook" apron and keeping an eye on burgers that smelled like heaven. Her mom was chopping vegetables for a salad, while Sarah poured drinks. Ben was setting the table.

"Just in time," her mom said when Meg came through the mudroom door. "Colton came looking for you here. Did you find each other—"

Meg tried to cover the hole in her coat with her hand, but it was too late. Her mom's gaze flicked to it right away, then up to Meg's face. Meg watched as her mom's expression went flat. It was the look she and her siblings feared the most—when their mom was too upset to even react.

Her mom shook her head so slightly that no one else noticed. *We'll talk about this later,* she mouthed to Meg, who nodded her understanding and swallowed hard. She hung up her coat and slid off her boots, but she'd suddenly lost her appetite.

Her face hot with shame, Meg went to the sink and washed her hands. There was a pit in her stomach the size and shape of the hole in her coat sleeve. She could see the price tag dangling from the jacket when she first spotted it in the mall—how many Christmas trees did her parents have to sell to make that much? How long had they stashed away a few dollars here or there to buy it for her?

Just when she thought she couldn't possibly feel any worse, Meg was struck by a terrible thought. What if her mom figured out that a dog had ripped her jacket? Would she lose any shot she had of convincing her parents to let her keep Chestnut? This would all be so much easier if she didn't have to keep Chestnut a secret.

Meg volunteered to get the ketchup and mustard from the fridge, which she took as an opportunity to wipe away the tears that filled her eyes. By the time they sat down around the dinner table, Meg was filled to the brim with anxiety, leaving no room for her dad's burgers. Her mind whirring with thoughts of how she would explain the ripped coat, Meg heard her family talking as if from afar.

"How's the physics studying going, Sarah?" her dad asked as he squirted ketchup onto his bun.

Sarah sighed. "It's okay, but I'm a little worried about the short-answer part."

Their dad nodded, but Ben scoffed.

"I'm sure you'll be fine," Ben said, rolling his eyes and taking a ridiculously large bite of salad. Sarah was excellent at science, and she'd never gotten less than a B+ on any test. "The bigger news," Ben went on, "is that basketball tryouts are next week. There are a bunch of new freshmen, so I might have to fight for my spot this year."

It was Sarah's turn to roll her eyes. Ben might not have been great at physics, but he was the high scorer on the varsity basketball team. "You're the team captain," Sarah said between bites of her burger. "You know that, right?"

"You never know," Ben said, failing to keep a straight face. "They might be so good they kick me off the team."

Meg's dad gave Ben a playful whack on the shoulder.

"And you, Megs," her dad said. "How is school going for you?"

"Why don't you like dogs, Daddy?" Meg blurted, changing the subject.

The room went quiet. Her dad cleared his throat.

"Don't ask, Micro," Ben said, breaking the awkward silence. "Trust me, I've tried."

But Meg looked from her dad to her mom. "Can we *please* get one? I'll do all the work. I'll feed him and take him on walks. And if you need me to earn money to afford him, I can, I promise."

A muscle tightened in her dad's jaw. "No. And that's a firm no."

Meg's face went hot with anger. Her dad had

dismissed her without even giving her a reason. He was treating her like the baby once again.

After a moment, her dad, Ben, and Sarah picked up their chatter about sports and school, friends and business. Meanwhile, Meg and her mom ate without speaking. Meg felt even more terrible, and her mom's silence was nearly too much to bear. She picked at her burger, the greasy meat sitting heavily in her stomach.

After they had cleaned up the kitchen, her dad went upstairs to take a shower, Sarah went to her room to study, and Ben left to play video games with his friends. Meg found herself alone with her mom as her heart pounded in her chest. She didn't want to have the talk she knew was coming, but at the same time she wanted to get it over with. She couldn't take the dread anymore.

Her mom let out a long, tired sigh. "Are you going to tell me what happened to your coat?" she asked, sitting down heavily on the couch.

"I'm so sorry—" Meg started, searching for the right words. "I . . . I got it caught on the fence. I . . . I shouldn't have climbed over it. But I'll fix it . . . I promise." She sat down beside her mom. "I really am so sorry." The lie felt like a lump of stone in her mouth, and Meg almost spilled the truth right then and there. But Chestnut's face passed through her mind and she pushed aside her guilt. She looked down at her lap and squeezed her eyes shut, waiting for the tongue-lashing she knew was coming—and that she deserved.

To Meg's surprise, her mom was quiet. "I know, Meggie," she finally said, her voice more exhausted than exasperated. She didn't say anything else for a long moment, and it dawned on Meg that her mom was upset about more than the coat. With a hot jolt of guilt, Meg realized that she'd been so distracted by Chestnut that she'd forgotten how many concerns her family had about the farm. The coat was the least of their problems.

Meg hugged her mom. "I really want to help—I can do more around the lot and I'll make more ornaments and I can try to sell more cookies and anything else you need."

Her mom kissed the top of Meg's head. "Thank you, sweetie. But it's not your job to worry—that's for me and Dad to do. I just wish things weren't so tough. I wish . . . well, I wish a lot of things." Her mom let out a dry laugh. "But the thing is, between the spider spruce mites and more people using artificial trees now, well . . ." She trailed off and was quiet for a moment before continuing. "The thing is, I don't think we can afford to keep the staff. Daddy and I are talking about having to let them go, and it breaks our hearts."

Meg felt like someone had kicked her in the stomach. The workers on the tree farm had been with their family for years. Some of them had worked for her parents for Meg's whole life. One of the foremen, Mr. Mike, had worked for Briggs Family Tree Farm since Meg's dad was a little boy, when her grandma and grandpa had still owned the farm. The idea of all of them leaving felt impossible. With Christmas coming, it felt like a cruel joke.

"Isn't there anything we can do?" Meg said desperately.

Her mom pulled her closer. "I don't want you to worry about it, Meggie. We've been through a lot of hard times before, and this will pass too. You don't need to figure out a way to fix this, sweetheart. It isn't your job. Your job is to be a kid and enjoy yourself while you can. We've never wanted you to have any kind of heartache. But it looks like we might have failed at that." Her mom's eyes began to fill with tears, and Meg had to look away to keep herself from crying.

Her mom ran her fingers through Meg's thick hair, which was tangled from running around in the woods with Colton and Chestnut. Meg wanted to remind her mom that she was big enough to help now, but she sat quietly, nestled in the crook of her mom's arm. She knew that there was nothing she could say to ease her parents' problems, and sometimes a hug was the best you could offer.

Her mom pulled away from Meg a little to look at her. "You know why we never got another dog?" her mom asked, as if she could read her mind.

Meg was intrigued, but she tried to act calm. "Why?"

"When Bruiser got old, things got harder on all of us. Sure, there were the vet bills, and the extra stress of caring for an old dog. But your dad loved that dog so much, and Bruiser loved your dad. In fact, Bruiser loved your dad more than anyone."

"Really? I thought Dad didn't like dogs at all."

Her mom shook her head. "Bruiser was a good dog, and really smart. Whenever a car pulled into the tree lot, Bruiser would greet the family. He'd help your dad around the farm, dragging dead trees over to the woodchipper and grabbing things for him when they were out of reach. He even helped sniff out those blasted spruce mites in the off season." Her mom sighed. "Your dad and Bruiser were an inseparable pair."

Meg's breath caught in her chest. She couldn't imagine how sad her dad must have been when Bruiser died. "But if Bruiser was such a help around the farm, why can't we get another family dog?"

"Well, when he died, it was like losing a family member. You kids were all so little — Sarah was only seven at the time — that it didn't hit you as hard. But your dad mourned that dog for months, years even. I guess you could say he's still mourning, in many ways."

"Are you afraid that if we get another dog Dad will be sad again?" Meg asked, her voice trembling.

Her mom nodded. "Yes, Meggie. And no. The main reason we've never considered it is because of you kids. You're all older now, and if we were to get another family pet, it would affect all of us. Every decision we've ever made has been to give you three the best life we could, and I'd love for you to know how great it is to have a dog. But I don't think I could bear to see you hurting if anything happened to it. Plus now it's been so long, I'm afraid your dad will never be able to love another dog again."

Meg's stomach dropped.

The truth hit her square in the chest. It wasn't that her parents didn't think she was responsible enough to take care of a dog. It wasn't even about the money it would cost to have one. The truth was that they were trying to spare her the pain of falling in love with a pet and having her heart broken when she lost him.

But little did they know that Meg was already in love with a dog. And she was already faced with the possibility of losing him. Now she had an even bigger problem. Even if everything went right with her ornament plan, what if her dad still turned Chestnut away? For that to happen now, after everything . . . Meg couldn't finish the thought. She just had to hope it wouldn't come to that.

★ CHAPTER 12 ★

Early the next morning, Meg forced herself from beneath her covers. The sun was just rising above the horizon and a rime of frost clung to the windowpane. Meg yawned and groped for her fluffy robe.

She had stayed up late again, making sixty more ornaments. She wanted to be sure she had some new stock before the ladies from city hall came to look at them. She didn't know if it would be enough, but it was a start.

Since she was a toddler, Meg's Sundays had always been reserved for Gigi—her grandma. When Meg's parents had taken over the farm, her dad's mom had given them the main house, where they lived now. She had moved to a smaller house at the edge of the farm, and she was famous around town for her crafting skills —not to mention her baking.

Meg was hoping Gigi could be helpful with her current, slightly overwhelming project. She gathered her materials and dumped them into her backpack. If Gigi would help, they'd get a ton of work done together. Meg was sure of it.

She stuffed her backpack with supplies and dressed extra warmly, since the bike ride to Gigi's was likely to be a cold one. Meg tiptoed down the stairs and into the kitchen. She grabbed a granola bar for herself and then rummaged through the refrigerator, looking for a treat she could bring Chestnut. She stumbled upon a few hard-boiled eggs and a ziplock bag with several pieces of bacon left over from Saturday's breakfast. But just as she was stuffing the bag into her coat pocket, her dad entered the kitchen, bleary-eyed and still in his pajamas.

"Hey, Meggie. What's the rush?" He nodded at the baggie in her hand. "You don't want to heat that bacon up and eat it warm?"

Meg shook her head, the now familiar guilt for telling a lie churning in her belly before she even told it. "No thanks. I don't mind it cold. I really want to get to Gigi's and get busy on the ornaments. Plus, she said we could bake cookies, too!"

Her father nodded. "You want me to get dressed and drive you over?"

Meg nearly choked on her reply. She couldn't get a ride—she had to go feed the dog that her dad didn't know she was hiding . . . and that he didn't want her to have. "That's okay. I need to gather up some more pinecones on the way. Thanks though."

"Suit yourself," her dad said as he fumbled with the coffee filter. "Call us if you decide you want a ride home."

"Will do. Love you." Meg pulled on her gloves and backpack.

"Love you, too," her dad called out just before she pulled the side door shut behind her. "Be safe."

Meg's guilty conscience weighed more than her backpack. She tromped through the snow to the barn and got her bike, then rode to the end of the drive.

Hoping that her father was no longer watching her, she turned in the opposite direction from her grandma's house. It was the *right* way to get to Chestnut, who she was pretty sure was waiting impatiently for his breakfast.

At the shed, Meg unlatched the door to find an enthusiastic and very hungry Plott hound. Chestnut leaped on her happily, licking her face and wiggling with joy. But the moment she told him to sit, he did.

Chestnut sat like a statue while she opened the bag of bacon, and when she offered a piece, he waited until she said "Go ahead" before gobbling it down in one quick bite. Meg took her time, feeding him the five strips of leftover bacon and the eggs. Then she took him outside so he could get a bit of exercise before she left.

They chased each other through the woods, Meg laughing as Chestnut ran in circles around her, herding her along in the early morning light. They collected pinecones until the extra tote bag she had brought was completely full. Out of breath, she stopped and dug a bottle of water out of her backpack. She took a long swig then poured some into her hand for Chestnut. He slurped it from her palm and licked the droplets from his mouth when he was done.

They stood there together, under the soft sun, while the woods woke up around them. Meg's breath turned to steam on the chilly air. Chestnut's ears twitched at the sound of every bird tweeting at its babies to get up or chipmunk foraging in the icy underbrush. Meg gazed up toward the sky at the tops of the trees rising all around them, and Chestnut leaned against her leg.

She loved it here, and she'd never known her favorite spot in the world could get even better with her dog by her side.

Once the bird chorus had reached peak volume, Meg knew it was time to get going. "I'm so sorry, Chestnut, but I have to go. Come on, boy." She headed back to the shed and Chestnut walked along beside her, entering the dark building without hesitation and sitting at attention. His tail thumped against the ground as she gave him a couple of treats and a kiss on the snout.

When Meg tried to shut the door, locking him back

in, Chestnut barked wildly. He scratched at the door and whined and barked. His hoarse voice sounded so sad that Meg's heart actually hurt as she listened to it.

Now Meg's guilt had doubled. Not only did she feel terrible about lying to her parents, but she also felt ashamed that Chestnut had to live in a tiny, musty shed. She had to do something to remedy both situations—soon.

But she just needed a little more time.

"Just hang on for me," she said through the wooden slats. "Okay, Chestnut?" The dog only whimpered in response, and Meg forced herself to walk away.

As soon as she rode up to the house, Meg knew that a day with Gigi was just what the doctor ordered. She didn't seem to mind that Meg had shown up late. In fact, she had Meg's favorite lunch, grilled cheese, waiting for her on the cast iron skillet.

"Nutmeg!" Gigi exclaimed. "You're here! I was about to start on the Christmas cookies."

They spent the rest of the afternoon elbow deep in paint and beads, cookie dough and frosting. Meg had been right. Making ornaments with her grandma's help really was faster—and easier. She could churn out ornaments at twice the speed Meg could, and she showed Meg ways to streamline the painting and decorating process.

Gigi had even offered to sew up the hole in Meg's new coat, which made Meg feel a little better, since her grandma was the best seamstress in town. Meg told her the same story about snagging her sleeve on the fence, and Gigi nodded knowingly.

"Psh," she said, smiling as she nearly crossed her eyes to thread the needle with shiny purple thread. "I can't tell you how many times your daddy came home with holes bigger than that in his coat sleeves, his jeans—heck, even his shoes." Gigi laughed at the memory. "If you can name it, he tore it. And not just on fences, either. Climbing trees, rolling down hills, wrestling with his dog."

Her grandma bent over the torn sleeve.

"I didn't even think he *liked* dogs. Mom just told me yesterday," Meg said.

Gigi looked up from her tidy stitches. "He sure did. For a while, anyway." Her mouth arced downward into a frown. "Broke his heart when Bruiser died." Her grandma studied Meg's face intently, as if she was searching for some kind of message there.

Meg squirmed in her seat, and for an instant she considered telling her everything. But she hesitated and the moment passed. Gigi looked back down at her sewing.

When the tear was repaired so perfectly it was almost invisible, Meg's grandma said, "Well, now. Let's turn on some holiday songs and really get this party started." Meg ran to start a CD, and they sang "Jingle Bell Rock" until they were hoarse. The smell of fresh-baked cookies filled the air.

Between them, they transformed dozens and dozens of plain-looking pinecones into simple but elegant ornaments. Gigi turned some of the wider ones into brightly painted zinnias, and Meg dotted hers with colors that looked like strings of tree lights. When they finished, Meg looked around the pinecone-laden table in awe and calculated how much money she could make if all the ornaments sold.

"Shall I make us an early dinner, sweetheart?"

her grandma asked as she washed the paint from her hands.

Meg's stomach gurgled at the suggestion. "Yes, please! Can we have potato soup?"

"Of course," Gigi replied, pulling the last tray of cookies from the oven. "With milk, I presume?"

Meg couldn't help but grin. Potato soup with milk was her grandma's specialty, a meal she only made around Christmastime. It was the perfect dish to share on such a cozy day. As her grandma heated up the soup and Meg spread butter on toast, Meg heard a familiar sound in the distance.

At first, she thought she must be imagining it, but her grandma looked out the kitchen window, toward the sound. "Is that a dog barking?" she asked, wiping her hands on a kitchen towel and pushing aside the curtains. "Well, would you look at that."

Suddenly nervous, Meg peered out the window. Outside, running in circles around her parked bicycle, was Chestnut, his nose pressed to the ground as he searched for her—and barked.

"Oh, no," Meg said under her breath. She looked

furtively at her grandma. "That's one of Colton's dogs. He must have gotten out of the yard."

"Is it now?" her grandma asked, her eyebrows rising on her forehead.

Meg pulled on her boots and ran out to Chestnut. Behind her, her grandma stood in the doorway. At the sight of Meg, Chestnut stood up on his hind legs and swatted at the air. He looked like he was dancing.

When she got closer, Meg said "sit" in a firm voice, and Chestnut immediately sat at attention. His tail wagged back and forth on the ground, making a mini snow angel. Meg patted his head and squatted down so they were eye to eye.

"What are you doing here?" she asked him quietly. "And how did you get out of the shed?"

In response, he whimpered excitedly and snapped his mouth open and shut in a silent bark. He could barely contain his glee at seeing her again. It would have been adorable if it weren't so risky, Meg thought. She held out her hand, palm first and fingers pointed upward. "Stay, Chestnut." She turned to go back to the house but made the mistake of looking back over her shoulder. Chestnut took that as a cue to follow her, and he ran after her, looking a little frantic.

Meg spun around to face him. "Chestnut!" she groaned, glad her back was to her grandma's questioning gaze. "Stay. Stay here!" She turned around again, and Chestnut whined loudly.

Gigi chuckled. "Looks like if you're going to get any soup, we're going to have to let that dog come in, too."

"Really?" Meg asked, heart in her throat. "Is that okay? Otherwise, I could take him home to . . . to Colton's."

Her grandma smiled coyly, her bright eyes flashing. "You know, for a dog that belongs to someone else, this Chestnut sure seems attached to you." Then without another word, she opened the door wide and let them both into her kitchen.

Once inside, Chestnut stuck to Meg's side, as if he were afraid she'd disappear if he lost sight of her. And even though Meg loved having him with her all afternoon, she felt queasy as the lies stacked up. Her grandma kept asking her questions about Chestnut, and Meg fumbled for a story.

According to her fib, Colton's family had just gotten Chestnut from a family friend who didn't need a tracking dog anymore, and they were still working on training him. That's why he must have run away and found her. Meg allowed herself to tell one truth about Chestnut: she told her grandma that he had an issue with separation anxiety that they were working on.

"I'll say!" Gigi nodded at Chestnut, who lay on top of Meg's feet, preventing her from moving.

Meg felt like the whole situation was spinning out of control. Every time she had to tell another lie about Chestnut, the story got bigger and harder to manage. She had never lied to her family before — especially her grandma. It felt as if she'd broken something that couldn't be fixed.

By the time Meg climbed on her bike, she was convinced she could never make it all better. Even if she somehow convinced her parents to let her keep

Chestnut, she'd eventually have to come clean to Gigi, which now gave her a whole new thing to worry about.

Her grandma leaned against the doorway, watching Meg and Chestnut head down the driveway. Meg paused before turning onto the road that crossed through their property and looked back. She waved at her grandma, who blew her a kiss in response. Meg pedaled as fast as she could to stay warm. As she rode, she looked down at the dog trotting alongside her and sighed. Chestnut stayed close to her bike, even without a leash. He seemed blissfully unaware of the heaviness of Meg's heart. She wished she could feel as carefree as he did.

Meg longed for a time when things had been simpler, and she didn't have to worry about getting caught in the web of lies she'd somehow woven.

★ CHAPTER 13 ★

Meg sped into Colton's yard with Chestnut tight on her heels. They were immediately surrounded by Colton's dogs—barking, jumping, and wildly excited to see them both. Chestnut froze, and the fur on his back stood up. Meg could tell that he wasn't being aggressive—he was afraid of the pack of high-energy farm dogs.

Meg patted his head as she dismounted from her bike. "Go ahead," she said, urging him to play. She was in the process of greeting each of Colton's dogs when she heard the farmhouse door swing open. She looked up to see Colton pulling on his coat as he crossed the yard.

"Hey!" he said. His eyes widened when he saw Chestnut. "Uh, what's he doing here?"

Meg sighed. "He escaped from the shed and tracked me to Gigi's house. I had to lie and say he was one of your dogs."

Colton looked at Meg, and she knew that he didn't approve of her lying again. But Chestnut sidled over to him and happily received Colton's ear scratches. The other dogs were giving Chestnut the once-over with their noses. At first the Plott hound tensed up, but after a moment, he shyly sniffed at Bentley. His ears twitched as Bentley sniffed him back, but then Bentley splayed his front legs and lowered his chest to the ground, letting Chestnut know he wanted to play. Next Mya, the German shepherd mix, lunged at Chestnut playfully and he jumped backwards. He shot her some side-eye, then decided he wanted to play, too.

Chestnut barked and half lunged at Mya, then scurried away, inviting her to chase him. They ran in a circle around the yard, and soon Bentley joined in and chased them both.

"What's your plan, Meg?" Colton asked.

"I honestly don't know," Meg said, watching the dogs play. "He's going to get me in trouble if he keeps escaping, but I feel so bad keeping him locked up in the shed. It isn't fair to him. I just feel like I'm failing at everything, Colt." She bit her lip to keep her feelings from spilling over, but she couldn't fight it. "What if Chestnut can't be trained? What if he's always going to be anxious when I'm not around? What if he'll never stay put? What if the ornaments bomb and I can't afford to keep him after all? What if I get caught lying before I have a chance to tell my mom and dad and grandma the truth? What if . . ." She trailed off, because there were just too many *what ifs* to count.

"What if," Colton said, punching her lightly on the shoulder, "everything works out fine?"

Meg looked over, her eyes wide. "Does that mean that you're going to help me?"

Colton shrugged. "I might have decided to switch strategies. Listen, worrying isn't going to help. My grandpa always says, 'Worrying is just borrowing trouble,' and he's right. You've already told a lie—"

"A lot of lies," she said with a pained look.

"Okay, a lot of lies. Right now, your best bet is to try to train Chestnut to be the perfect farm dog."

Meg's shoulders sagged. "I know you're right. I just . . . I don't want to lose him. I know I've only had him for a couple days, but he's already . . . I don't know . . . It's corny, but Chestnut feels like family."

At the sound of his name, Chestnut stopped wrestling with Mya. He looked at Meg and popped up to standing, waiting for her command. Meg knelt down and hugged her dog. Chestnut nestled gently into her shoulder, his nose pressed against her as if he were hugging her back.

Colton clicked his tongue and all of his dogs sat, waiting for his command. Chestnut looked at them, confused at first, then followed their lead. Meg smiled. She knew in her heart that Chestnut could be trained to help out on the farm. She knew that he was a good dog, and that he was meant to be hers. She just didn't know how to make it all happen yet.

"To me," Colton said, gesturing to his dogs. Moving as a pack, they ran to him and sat at attention. Chestnut trailed after them and sat down too.

"Good," Colton said, passing out a round of dog biscuits from his pocket. Meg had never known a time when Colton didn't have a pocket full of dog treats. It was one of a million reasons why he was the coolest person she knew.

"Lie down," Colton said. All six of his dogs lay down. They were practically drooling for treats, but Colton waited patiently until Chestnut lay down as well. Then he passed out another round of dog biscuits. "Good work, team," he said, praising each of them with a pat.

"Roll over," Colton said, moving his finger in a circular motion as he spoke. Four of his dogs rolled over immediately, while Mya rolled onto her back and wiggled like she had an itch. Bella stood up on her hind legs and danced in a little circle. Colton managed to keep a straight face, but Meg laughed at her silly moves.

"Not like that, Bella," Colton said, his voice firm. He gave a treat to each of the dogs that had rolled all the way over, then stood in front of Mya. "Mya, roll over," he said, repeating the hand signal. This time

Mya rolled all the way over and wagged happily as she took her treat from Colton's fingertips.

"Bella, roll over," Colton said. The dog looked at him for a moment, as if she were deciding whether or not she felt like behaving. Then she rolled over, just as the others had done.

"That's a good girl, Bella," Colton said, reaching down to pet her as she calmly took her biscuit. Colton sat down on the steps. Bella lay down next to him and put her front paws on his lap.

"Now you try with Chestnut," he said to Meg, tossing her a treat.

Meg stood in front of her dog, who watched her with a curious—and slightly confused—expression. "Chestnut," Meg said, making the circular gesture. "Roll over."

Chestnut flopped onto his side, watching Meg carefully. "Encourage him," Colton suggested.

"That's a good start," Meg said to Chestnut. "Good boy. Now roll over!" Chestnut flipped onto his back, wiggled happily for a moment with his paws in the air, then slowly flopped over onto his opposite side.

"Give him the treat," Colton said, grinning. "It wasn't pretty, but it was a roll."

Meg scratched Chestnut's ears. She held out a treat, and he hopped to his feet in a flash to accept his reward. "He's a smart dog, isn't he, Colt?"

"Totally," Colton said. He considered the dog carefully. "I think he's just really freaked out because he was abandoned. He needs to know that you're not going to leave him too." Colton walked over to Chestnut, who swept his tail across the ground.

Meg knew what it felt like to be anxious. Sometimes, when she lay in bed at night thinking about how worried her parents seemed all the time, she felt her heart beat faster. She couldn't stop her mind from jumping to the worst possible outcome—what if they lost the farm? What if they had to move? In those moments, she felt helpless and scared, like the whole world was closing in.

She understood why Chestnut felt that way, but it was awful to think of him being so frightened. No matter how many times Meg's parents told her not to worry, she couldn't stop herself. It was the same for

Chestnut—so how would she ever get him to believe that she wouldn't abandon him too?

"I just—" Meg fumbled for the right words. "Where do I even start? Even if I could get Chestnut to believe that I'm always going to be there for him, what if . . . what if my parents don't let me keep him?" Her eyes filled with tears. "And I just end up abandoning him like the last person he loved?"

Colton shook his head sadly. He picked up a stray tennis ball and threw it. The herd of dogs went chasing after it, barking and tripping over one another. "Right now, all you can do is try not to let that happen, okay? You've got to focus on helping Chestnut become a great farm dog. I've got some training books you can read, and you're going to work with him as hard as you can. Everything else will work itself out." Chestnut trotted back to them, carrying the tennis ball. Colton took it from his mouth and lightly thumped the dog on the side. "I just know it will."

"Thanks, Colt." Meg wiped her eyes and took a deep breath. Right then and there, she believed Colton was right. He just had to be.

★ CHAPTER 14 ★

Meg walked Chestnut back to the shed as the sun started to go down. The closer they got to the ramshackle wooden building, the more she was filled with dread. How was she going to keep him locked in all night? He'd proven that he was able to escape and track her down. What if she woke up in the morning to find him on their lawn? Or at the Christmas tree lot? What would she tell her parents then?

When they got to the shed, Meg saw that her fears were for nothing. Chestnut was completely worn out from his playdate with Colton's dogs. He ambled right inside and headed straight for the horse blankets, which he now knew were his bed. He spun in a circle and scratched at the fabric, looking for the most comfortable spot before settling down, curling himself into a little doughnut shape and resting his head on his paws.

Meg sat down on the ground next to him. She patted her knees, and Chestnut looked up at her. He raised his head and gently laid it in her lap. Then he laid his paw over her arm, like a dog version of a hug.

She leaned her head against the wall for a moment and absently traced the brindle stripes on Chestnut's silky fur. *Chestnuts roasting on an open fire . . .* she hummed. *Jack Frost nipping at your nose . . .* Here in the shed with her dog, Meg felt peaceful and safe.

Chestnut had fallen asleep to her lullaby. He snored softly, and Meg smiled.

After a moment, he made a soft woofing sound in his sleep. His legs moved as if he was running. She wondered what he was dreaming about. Was he playing with Mya or tracking a squirrel? Chasing Meg or barking at trucks? She curled herself around him, breathing in the smell of his warm fur and puppy breath. She wished that she could stay like this forever.

Here in the shed, there was no room for anxiety or fear. She didn't have to try to prove herself to her family. She didn't have to try to help save the farm. In here, she felt peaceful and safe. Chestnut was already hers, and they could just be together.

Despite the musty straw, dirt floor, and wind blowing outside, the shed was cozy. Meg and Chestnut were snuggled together for warmth. She was going to head home soon—very soon—but first she just wanted to close her eyes . . . only for a minute . . .

Meg woke to the sound of morning songbirds, louder than they normally were. Her stomach grumbled as her eyes popped open. At first she was disoriented —where was she? This wasn't her bedroom, and she wasn't in her soft bed. She shivered and realized she was lying on something damp and hard. Her back hurt. And what was Chestnut doing here? The dog had woken up when she did, his tail wagging like crazy before his eyes were even open.

Chestnut . . . not her bed . . . the cold . . . Meg jumped to her feet, suddenly wide awake—and suddenly all too aware of where she was. She was in the shed. With Chestnut. And it was morning—she'd spent the whole night there! Had her parents realized she was gone? Had her whole family been looking for her? She had to get home. Meg ran for the door but stopped with her hand on the latch.

She turned back to look at Chestnut, who was up on his feet, looking at her with a confused expression. His ears were up and his head was cocked to the side, as if to say, *Where are you going?*

Meg gulped. "Chestnut—I'm so sorry, but I have to go! I'll be back. I promise." She turned to the door and heard the dog whine. She squeezed her eyes shut. What if Chestnut wouldn't let her go?

Then she remembered what Colton had said.

She had to make sure Chestnut knew that she'd always come back. She turned to look at him, and he started wagging his tail again.

If only she could make Chestnut trust that she was always thinking of him—and feel like she was with him all the time. Meg squinted through the slats in the wall and saw that the sun hadn't quite peeked over the horizon. She guessed it was about five o'clock in the morning. Her mom and dad wouldn't be up for a little while yet. Maybe she'd get lucky—maybe they had fallen asleep early and not realized she was gone.

Maybe she had just a bit of time to work with Chestnut before she went home.

"Come on, Chestnut. Let's go for a little walk." The dog leaped up, ready and willing to follow Meg wherever she led. His tail was going like crazy, and he pressed his warm nose into Meg's hand, looking for a morning scratch. She tickled him behind the ears and under his chin, and his mouth turned up in a furry smile. He let out a happy snort as he trotted over to the door of the shed and scratched at it.

"All right, you," Meg said. The door creaked, and he ran past her out into the gray dawn.

The air was crisp, and Meg's lungs stung as she breathed in the morning cold and exhaled puffs of steam. Several more inches of snow had fallen overnight. They walked through the woods for a few minutes, the crunch of Meg's boots the only sound around them. Chestnut sniffed the ground, his tail straight out behind him as he searched for something. Suddenly he froze, his ears up and back, his front legs slightly splayed, and his eyes intently focused on something Meg couldn't see.

Out of the corner of her eye, Meg spotted a tiny shadow scurrying by. Chestnut barked excitedly and leaped like a bucking bronco, chasing a terrified field mouse that was running for its life.

"Shhh! Chestnut—you're going to wake up the whole town!" At the sound of her voice, Chestnut snapped his mouth shut and zipped back to her side. Meg giggled. "Did you have to scare the life out of that poor little thing?" The dog blinked at her, as if he could convince her of his innocence. She burst out laughing.

Meg thought back to one of the dog training books she and Colton had looked at before she left. In the first chapter, the trainer who wrote it said that you shouldn't make a big deal out of coming and going. Acknowledging the dog as you're leaving or when you return will just increase his anxiety.

Meg took a deep breath. "Chestnut, come." He

followed her back to the shed without hesitation. She opened the door, and Chestnut trotted inside. Without a word, she closed the door behind him, walked about ten feet away, and stood still, waiting. From inside the shed came the soft, sad sound of whining. Meg bit her lip and forced herself to ignore it. After several long moments, when the whining had died down, she went back to the door and opened it. Her heart swelled when she saw Chestnut standing just on the other side, his eyes full of worry. She wanted to scoop him up in her arms, but Meg steeled herself and, following the book's directions, didn't acknowledge or pet the dog. Instead, she left the door open, spun around, and walked away, letting Chestnut choose whether to follow her or not.

Of course, he did. She walked back into the woods while he wandered nearby, sniffing to his heart's content. When he was staring intently at some kind of critter scratching under a downed tree branch, Meg knew he wasn't focused on her. She wanted to reward him, so she slipped him a treat and scratched him behind the ears. He glanced at her quickly, half wagged his tail, then turned back to his target.

"Good boy," Meg praised him.

While he was distracted, Meg picked up a stick. She whistled to get Chestnut's attention, and his head shot toward the sound. She held the stick out in front of her as he watched it closely, anticipation on his face. Meg drew her arm back over her shoulder, then threw it as hard as she could. It arced off into the trees, and Chestnut bolted after it.

She smiled to herself. That hadn't gone so badly. He had whined, but then he'd calmed down. He'd followed her but hadn't been hyperfocused on her—he'd been interested in other things, as if he trusted that she would still be nearby.

Chestnut galloped back with the stick and dropped it in front of her. She rewarded him with a treat, which he wolfed down in one swallow before pawing at the ground to tell her to throw the stick again.

"Sit," Meg said. He sat down and looked up at her expectantly. "Good boy."

He stayed seated but bobbed his snout up and down as he caught a scent on the breeze. Meg held out a hand to pet him, and he buried his nose in her palm, sniffing it furiously. Something she'd read in the book came back to her—that when a dog and owner are really bonded, the dog can sometimes be soothed by an item that smells like the owner, like a piece of clothing. She didn't know if it would work, but it couldn't hurt.

Meg unwound the rainbow-striped scarf from her neck—the one her mom had knitted for her over the summer—and crouched down in front of Chestnut. She held it out for him to sniff. He ran his nose along the rows of yarn, inhaling repeatedly, then exhaling with a snort to clear his nostrils. His tail started to wag.

"I'm going to put this on you," she said. "It smells like me, so maybe you'll always feel like I'm close by, okay?" Meg wrapped the scarf loosely around his neck. A frantic look in his eyes, the dog tried to back out of the soft but strange contraption around his neck. When it moved with him he swiped at it, getting his paw stuck in it. He tried to pull his leg back, but his claws were tangled in the yarn. Whimpering, Chestnut spun around in a circle on three legs, trying to undo himself, until finally Meg wrapped her arms around him to stop him. He was shaking as she eased his paw out.

"Aw, Chestnut!" she said. "You're okay. It's just a scarf—it's not going to hurt you." She stroked his head. Chestnut blinked and sniffed at the scarf again, then stretched his face toward her and licked her cheek. Meg squeezed her eyes shut and giggled. "Thank you," she cooed. "I love you too."

Meg threw the stick a few more times, giving him a chance to use up his energy. She chased him in a zigzag through the trees, then squealed when he turned around and chased her right back. Panting and grinning, Meg led Chestnut back to the shed. She filled his food and water bowl and sat down next to him on a blanket. He promptly covered her in doggy kisses and lay down beside her.

It was getting late—Meg really needed to head home. Today was a school day.

Her parents would be waking up soon, and she

couldn't put it off any longer. She stood up, and the dog whimpered. Meg took a breath and reminded herself that staying tough now would help Chestnut in the long run. But that was hard to do when he was gazing up at her with those big, sweet—and sad—brown eyes.

"Chestnut, stay," she said firmly, pointing at the floor of the shed. "I'll be right back." She knew from Colton's book that it was important to have a cue word that she used whenever she was going to leave. Over time, Chestnut would associate those words with her leaving, but also her returning. She had decided that the phrase "I'll be right back" would work. For it to work, though, she had to mean it and stick to it. If she said she was coming back, she had to come back, otherwise he wouldn't trust her.

Chestnut kept looking at her, his eyes unblinking, but he didn't whimper and he didn't move. Meg backed out of the shed and into the brightening day. He stayed put, and Meg's chest nearly burst with happiness.

Sighing, Meg closed and latched the door, making sure that it was snug. She turned, and with one final glance at the shed, raced home, hoping against hope that her parents were still asleep.

Despite her fears, Meg was also feeling like her plan to be more grown-up was just starting to work. She was feeling helpful around the lot, and her parents were letting her do more and more work. She had made tons of ornaments, and if the lady from city hall came back, she'd have enough to sell her. She could feel that she and Chestnut were getting even closer and that he had started to trust her—and the more he trusted her, the calmer he got. Soon he would be the perfect dog.

Meg just had to keep doing exactly what she was doing. All of it. All the time.

Yes, she had a lot to do, and for a split second she started to feel overwhelmed. But Meg pushed away the feeling and told herself to focus on how far she had already come. If she worked hard enough and believed that she could do it, she would. She could do everything she—and Chestnut—needed.

★ CHAPTER 15 ★

Meg tiptoed up to the back door of the house and used the key hidden under the statue of a sleeping gnome to let herself in. She pulled the door closed and listened. The house was silent except for the steady ticking of the grandfather clock in the hallway. Meg held her breath as she crossed the kitchen and snuck through the living room. She was halfway across when she froze at the sound of footsteps above her. Her stomach dropped out, and she forced herself to remain calm.

Meg knew she only had a few seconds to get upstairs before her dad stumbled down to make coffee. She took the stairs two at a time—skipping the squeaky step—and moved as quickly and quietly as she could toward her room. Ben's snores seeped through his bedroom door. Sarah's alarm went off and Meg nearly jumped out of her skin. At the end of the hallway she heard her parents talking softly in their room.

"I'll make the coffee." Her father's voice had grown louder, and she heard the door knob rattle in his grip.

Meg ducked into her room and closed the door as fast as she could. She pulled off her jeans and tennis shoes and wrapped herself in her bathrobe. She needed to get into the shower before Sarah woke up —and before anyone got a good look at her. The scent of moldy shed and damp dog wafted off her clothes, and no matter how she tried, she couldn't think of any lies that would get her out of that.

She untangled her braid and opened the door, faking a yawn. As she crossed the hall, the door of Sarah's room flew open. Meg scooted past it and hustled to the bathroom.

"I call first shower," Meg said over her shoulder, shutting the door behind her. She crossed her fingers that Sarah hadn't managed to catch a glimpse of her face. She feared that guilt was written all over it.

The hot shower felt amazing after the cold night in the shed. Meg washed the smell of Chestnut out of her hair and the dirt from under her nails. When she had towel-dried her hair, brushed her teeth, and put on her bathrobe again, Meg stepped back into the hallway. Sarah brushed past her without a word, her face puffy from sleep and exhaustion.

Meg sighed as her bedroom door clicked shut behind her, her panic dissipating as she realized she'd gotten away with it. She dressed quickly and ran a comb through her hair, then headed downstairs for breakfast.

The morning was already in full swing. Her parents were ricocheting around the kitchen, stuffing cereal boxes back into cabinets and tossing milk cartons into the fridge. They were so busy they hardly noticed her standing there—let alone realized that she'd been gone all night. Meg felt horrible for lying and sneaking around, but she was equally full of something she hadn't been feeling much of lately: hope. She ate the cheese omelet that Ben offered to share with her. Then she scarfed down a blueberry muffin and a glass of milk.

She was just about to head back upstairs to grab her backpack when Sarah tromped into the kitchen and poured herself a cup of coffee while their mom and dad pulled on their boots. "Ready to hit the registers again, kiddo?" Sarah asked.

"What?" asked Meg, looking at her parents, who were already halfway out the door. "Today's a school day."

Sarah grabbed a muffin and followed Ben toward the door, headed for the truck. "Didn't you hear?" Sarah said. "Record snowfall last night. The whole district is closed for a snow day."

A snow day. Things really were starting to look up. Now, Meg would be able to track how well her ornaments were selling.

"Awesome," Meg said, calling out to them. "I'll clean up the dishes and head over in a minute."

Her sister nodded. Ben waved a hand in the air.

"See you later, Micro!" Ben called out from the driveway.

Sarah stopped in the doorframe and smiled at Meg. "Make sure you dry your hair before you go outside. You don't want to catch a chill."

Meg rolled her eyes at her sister. "Thanks, *Mom*," she shot back, and they both laughed as Sarah pulled the door closed behind her.

Meg cleaned up the kitchen and blow-dried her hair before pulling it into a tight braid. She tugged on her work boots and new purple coat—with its stitched-up sleeve—and trudged toward the tree lot, the Christmas carols growing louder over the fields as she got closer. By the time she got there, cars and trucks were already filling up the parking spaces, and the whole place was hopping with activity.

Ben was loading a tree onto the bed of a pickup truck while her dad pulled another one by the trunk through a short metal tube called the baler. The tree came out the other side wrapped in plastic netting, which flattened its branches and made it easier to transport. Her mom was working at the register and Sarah was filling the coffeemaker with water. In the distance, Meg could see several of the farm workers walking through the aisles with tree shoppers.

Several people were gathered around the baskets

full of ornaments. When Meg approached, her mom broke out into a big smile.

"Oh, here she is!" her mom said. "This is my daughter—she made the ornaments." Meg smiled sheepishly and gave a little wave.

"These are really beautiful," one woman said.

"You're so talented!" said another.

A man nodded approvingly. "Quite the artist, aren't you, young lady?"

"Oh, thanks!" Meg blushed. She stood there awkwardly for a second, not sure what else to say. She was relieved when they turned back to the ornaments and murmured to each other.

Meg moved to help a dad juggling two toddlers, a cup of hot chocolate, and a tree stand. She tried hard to ignore the fact that the three shoppers were still looking at her ornaments. They'd been there a long time, which made her feel anxious, embarrassed, and proud, all at once.

The morning flew by in a rush. Sales were especially good, and Meg began to let herself hope that this could be the day that turned things around for the farm. Maybe, just maybe, her parents had been wrong and they'd have the best Christmas season they'd ever had. Sarah interrupted Meg's daydream.

"Wow," Sarah said, giving her little sister a hip bump. Wisps of hair escaped her messy bun and her eyes flashed as she grinned. "We're having a great day today! Good job with those ornaments, Meggie."

"Thanks," Meg said. "I hope they help."

"Help? They're a huge hit!" Sarah looked up as more cars turned into the lot. "Gotta go," she said.

Sarah's words rang in Meg's head as she went about her work. She took payment from customers and refilled the cocoa pot. She put out fresh sugar cookies and straightened the wreaths. But even as busy as she was, she couldn't help but see that Sarah was right— the ornaments were selling really well, and the baskets were nearly empty. Meg worked through the afternoon with a smile on her face.

When there was a lull, Meg went into the stock trailer to catch her breath. Now that she had a quiet moment to herself, she realized she had barely slept in days, and she was truly exhausted. She sat down atop a stack of boxes and leaned her head against the wall. The storage trailer smelled like powdered cocoa mix, sugar cookies, baling twine, and the ever-present aroma of Fraser firs. It smelled so much like Christmas, which, Meg realized, smelled like home. The thought made her smile.

"Hey, Micro, wake up!" Someone shook her by the shoulder.

Meg jerked upright, eyes wide, and wiped drool from her cheek, trying to pretend she hadn't really fallen sound asleep in the stock trailer. "Oh, I . . . um . . ."

Ben was looking at her strangely, his brow scrunched together and his lips pursed. "What's going on with you?" he asked, sitting down next to her. "You seem really tired lately. You okay?"

Meg shook her head, trying to push her sleepiness aside. "Everything's great. I'm just . . . you know . . ." She trailed off.

Ben raised his eyebrows. "Micro, I'm your big brother. You can tell me anything."

She wanted badly to tell him the truth, just so that she wouldn't have to carry it around by herself. But she didn't know how.

"Thanks," she said, averting her gaze. "I'm just really tired from making ornaments."

"I don't buy it. I invented fudging the truth, so I know it when I see it." Ben shook his head. "You shouldn't have to work so hard. You should just be a kid."

And just like that, Meg was irritated again. Here she'd been feeling so proud of what she was contributing to the family, and Ben had to go and remind her that she was *just a kid*.

She stood up and glared at him. "I'm not a baby, Ben!" she spat. "I know all about what's happening with the farm, and I'm scared. Just like you are. Just like Mom and Dad and Sarah!" She put her hands on her hips and dared him to argue with her. "I'm a part of this family, too, and you guys don't need to protect me from the truth. You need to include me."

Ben raised his hands in surrender. "I didn't mean that, Micro. I just meant . . ." He fumbled for the right words. "I want you to know that we're here to help—*if* you need it." He looked away, embarrassed. "Besides, your ornaments are doing more to help the farm than I am."

Meg was surprised to see his face fall, and it took a second for her to understand that maybe he was feeling as helpless as she was.

"I'm sorry, I didn't mean—I just—"

"It's okay, Micro." Her brother flashed her a gloomy smile. "I mean *Meg*."

"Are we going to be okay?" Meg asked after a while, putting into words the question she'd wanted to ask for months.

"Yes," he said without a hint of doubt. "Absolutely. One hundred percent. No matter what happens, the family will be okay." He ruffled her hair, then said, "You're really not Micro anymore, huh?"

Ben chuckled, and Meg straightened her shoulders. Her brother was right about one thing. Meg wasn't Micro anymore. And it was time she started acting like she believed it herself.

★ CHAPTER 16 ★

The rest of the afternoon passed in a blur. As the sun was sinking in the sky and Meg was struggling with the large hot chocolate urn, Ben stopped next to her.

"Hey, Micro—I mean, Meg." He grinned. "Need some help?"

Meg's first instinct was to say no, but the urn was awkward and heavy and getting it off the table was hard for her. She felt a little sheepish, but she nodded. "Thanks, Ben."

Ben picked up the big container and moved it into the storage trailer. Then he and Meg washed it out together, letting the swirl of remaining cocoa drift down the drain. The family finished closing up the lot and climbed into the truck, each sighing tiredly.

"You guys hungry?" their mom asked over the roar of the ignition.

Meg laughed. "I don't think Ben is. He must have eaten thirty sugar cookies today."

Beside her, Ben snorted. "It wasn't thirty! And I'm still starving, anyway." He pinched Meg's arm but got mostly coat, and she stuck her tongue out at him.

"Maybe Ben needs to get up extra early and go help Miss Trudy bake the cookies," their dad said, grinning at them in the rearview mirror. Miss Trudy owned the local bakery and sold the tree farm hundreds of sugar cookies every holiday season.

Beside them in the back seat, Sarah shook her head and chuckled. "Ben's not allowed anywhere near Miss Trudy's ovens. He's banned for life after he ate a whole bowl of raw dough last time he went to 'help.'"

The family roared with laughter all the way home, while Ben boasted about his competitive-level cookie-eating ability.

"I'll show you," Ben said. "Tomorrow, I'll eat fifty!"

They pulled up to the house and tumbled out of the truck just as a soft snow began to fall. Meg, Ben, and Sarah giggled as they opened their mouths to catch the flakes.

They tromped single file into the mudroom, Ben bringing up the rear. They all unzipped their jackets and tugged off their boots, shaking out their stiff arms and legs.

The family fanned out into the house. Meg's parents went to the kitchen to start dinner, while Sarah headed upstairs to shower. Meg was still in the mudroom, straightening boots and tossing gloves into a big bin, when she heard a commotion outside. She opened the back door and looked out just in time to see Chestnut bursting out of the woods and into the yard. Meg's scarf hung from his mouth. It trailed behind him, dragging across the ground as he ran. Chestnut paused, dropped his nose to the ground, and sniffed frantically, like he was trying to pick up a scent. Then he took off again—racing straight for the house.

"What the . . . ?" Meg's mom had come back

into the mudroom. She stood right behind Meg, and together they watched Chestnut through the open door. Meg was frozen in shock and fear that her secret was about to be exposed, and her mom was frozen with total confusion at the sight of the enthusiastic pup.

Chestnut bounded right for them, and they reflexively stepped out of his way just in time as he leaped through the door without so much as a pause. He ran past them and skidded to a stop at Meg's dad's feet in the kitchen, his claws scraping on the smooth linoleum floor. Meg's dad stood still, holding a salad bowl in the air as if he had turned into a statue. He stared down at the dog with huge eyes and a shocked expression on his face. Meg and her mom hurried into the kitchen.

As soon as Chestnut spotted Meg, his whole body was bursting with joy. He hopped up and down in a happy dance, and his tail wagged so hard his whole body wagged with it. Meg didn't know what to do —just the sight of him made her smile, but she was filled with worry about how she was going to explain this to her parents. Should she pretend she didn't know the dog? And could she even get away with that when Chestnut was clearly so excited to see her?

Before she had time to formulate a plan, Chestnut ran right to Meg, jumped up and put his front legs on her stomach, and held out her scarf to her—as if he was just there to return it. Meg's heart thunked in her chest. There would be no getting out of this now. She'd been caught red-handed.

"Chestnut, down," she said. The dog lowered his front paws to the floor. "Sit." He sat.

Meg took a breath and turned to her parents, whose mouths hung open in confusion. Ben and Sarah had appeared in the doorway between the kitchen and living room, Sarah with her hand over her mouth and Ben shaking his head.

"Megan Lucille," her mom said, speaking quietly like she did when she was really upset. She pointed at Chestnut. "What. Is. This?"

Meg opened her mouth, still wondering if she should try to lie her way out of trouble. Just then, Ben knelt down beside Chestnut. He held the Plott hound's head in his hands and scratched him behind the ears, rubbing noses with him. Ben looked up at Meg with an expression of such love and understanding that tears came to her eyes. He nodded, as if to say, *I've got your back.* "Time to face the music, Meg."

Behind Ben, Sarah was smiling at Meg. She nodded too. Meg realized that her brother and sister had already put two and two together and knew that it equaled four paws.

They were right. It was time to come clean.

Meg turned back to her parents, who were looking at her like she'd grown a second head. She took a deep breath and, ignoring the tears that spilled from her eyes and ran under her chin, she forced herself to speak.

"Mom, Dad, this is Chestnut," Meg said. "He . . . he's my dog."

As hard as it was to get the words out, Meg was flooded with relief as soon as she said them. It felt so good to finally let out her huge secret.

"Your *what?*" her dad said, looking from her to Chestnut and back again. "You . . . we don't . . . A *dog?*"

"Meg, please. Tell us what's going on," her mom cut in.

"I found him a few days ago," Meg said, the words rushing out. "He was tangled up in the fence and he was just so scared and alone. And he was hurt. Colton and I treated his foot and I . . ." She didn't know how to say everything that she needed them to know. "I'm sorry that I lied, that I didn't tell you about him. But I love him, and he needs me. Look at him—he's so young and he doesn't have anyone else—he was just abandoned in the woods. Colton told me that happens a lot to hunting dogs, and Chestnut's an amazing tracker. He . . ."

Meg trailed off. Her mom was frowning, and her dad was looking grimly at Chestnut. Meg didn't know what that meant, so she swallowed hard and filled the tense silence with more words. "I'll take care of him. I'll even pay for his food and stuff. I can use the money from the ornaments to take care of him, as long as we have enough to pay the staff first."

Suddenly, all of Meg's worry and fear and love

for her family and for Chestnut came bursting to the surface.

"I just . . . I wanted to help," she said, her voice breaking. "I wanted to help you and the staff and the farm and Chestnut, and I wanted everyone to see that I could." As she told the truth, she began to feel lighter, like a weight was beginning to lift.

"I don't understand," her mom said, shaking her head. "How have you been keeping a dog?"

The disappointment on her mother's face was like a punch to Meg's gut, but she forced herself to look her mom in the eye. "He's been staying in the old shed, over in the western field," she said. Her mouth was dry, and a huge lump had formed in her throat. "I've been working with Colton to train him and I really think he could be a great farm dog. He's friendly and smart and he can track just about anything. He even tracked me to Gigi's house. He tracked me here, too." Meg looked at her parents. "Please, Mom, Dad. I'll never ask for anything else, ever again."

Her mom's face crumpled and she buried her face

in her hands. Her dad's normally twinkling eyes were full of anger and heartbreak. "Oh, Megs," he said. "We knew that you wanted a dog, but this . . . this is something else entirely."

Her mom looked up, her eyes brimming with tears. "It isn't just that you kept a dog when you knew it was against our wishes. And it isn't even that you kept a dog that wasn't rightfully yours, which was wrong, Meg."

The tone of her mom's voice made Meg feel nauseous. She'd never heard her so upset.

"Those things are both bad enough," her mom went on. "But, Meggie . . . you lied to us, and that isn't how this family works. We don't lie to each other. No matter what."

Meg looked down at the floor, then stared at Chestnut through watery eyes. Her dad cleared his throat, and when Meg looked up at him, he seemed so sad.

"When I told you that we couldn't get another dog, I meant it Meg," her dad said with a firm voice.

Meg let out a choked sob. She'd made the biggest mistake of her life, and there was no undoing it. She knew in her heart that her parents would never, ever let her keep Chestnut now.

At her feet, Chestnut sank to the floor with a whimper.

★ CHAPTER 17 ★

The family was silent as they climbed into the truck. Meg sat in the back seat between Ben and Sarah, with Chestnut curled on her lap. She could barely breathe as her dad put the truck into gear and backed out of the drive, turning toward town and the animal shelter.

Sarah squeezed one of Meg's hands gently, and Ben looped his arm through her elbow on the other side. But Meg only had eyes for Chestnut, who wiggled excitedly on her lap, straining to see out the window. He was so happy to be with the family. He had no idea what awaited him at the end of the drive. Meg was nearly overwhelmed with guilt, and she buried her face in his fur. After a few moments, Chestnut settled down, falling asleep with his head resting on Meg's arm.

Her worst fears had come true. Chestnut trusted her completely, and she was about to abandon him, just like his last owner had. Tears streamed down Meg's face as she struggled to believe that these were her final moments with her dog.

The closer they got to the shelter, the harder it was for Meg to hold back her sorrow. As they slowed to turn into the parking lot, a tiny cry escaped her mouth. Chestnut woke up immediately and hopped to his feet, his brow scrunched up with concern for her. He whined and licked at the tracks of her tears, and Meg's heart broke all over again. Sarah had also started to cry. Ben sat quietly, his pained gaze fixed on Chestnut's paw, which rested protectively on Meg's arm. Her dad glanced at her in the rearview mirror and her mom twisted in her seat to look at her. Their expressions were somber.

Her dad pulled into a parking spot and turned off

the ignition. The silence in the truck was awful. Sarah started to say something, but their mom reached out and put a hand on her knee to shush her.

"Come on, Meggie," their dad said wearily.

Meg felt like her boots weighed a hundred pounds each. She slid down out of the truck and called for Chestnut to follow her. He hopped out obediently and stuck close to her side all the way through the double glass doors into the shelter. Meg's family streamed in after them.

A television hung in the corner with the news playing on mute. Meg heard dogs barking somewhere in the distance, and Chestnut's ears shot up and forward as he tried to track the sound. He sniffed his way around the room.

Meg's dad approached the woman sitting behind the counter and began talking to her quietly. Meg's mom, Ben, and Sarah gathered around her. Meg looked at her mom.

"Can I—" Meg couldn't finish the sentence right away. She took a few quick breaths, waiting until she was able to speak without crying. "I need to say goodbye."

Her mom nodded sadly. Meg sat down on a bench in the far corner of the waiting room and clicked her tongue for Chestnut to join her, just like Colton had taught her. The dog trotted over and hopped up onto the bench next to her, looking at her so sweetly, so innocently, that Meg had to turn away for a second.

Meg leaned down and pressed her nose to his. "I'm so sorry, Chestnut," she said, her voice shaky. "But I have to leave you here. Everything's going to be all right, buddy, I promise." She gazed into his big, bright eyes. "You are the best dog ever, and you have made me so happy. But now it's time for you to make someone else happy."

She had promised him that she'd always come back. She had promised him that he would never be alone again. With a horrible pang, Meg realized that she hadn't just been lying to her family—she'd been lying to everyone. She'd lied to her parents, her siblings, her grandmother, and her best friend, but also to Chestnut—and especially to herself. She'd been so stupid to ever let herself think that this would work out.

She stroked his soft chin and ran a thumb along the dip in his forehead. She gently rubbed his ears, and he closed his eyes. "I love you, Chestnut," she whispered. "And I'll never, ever forget you. That's one promise I know I'll never break, as long as I live." Chestnut responded by licking her nose.

Meg looked over at her family, who stood huddled together at the front. Her dad had his face buried in his hands, and her mom had her arms wrapped around his shoulders. Meg couldn't help but think about Bruiser, and how her dad had never wanted any of his children to feel this way. Maybe being a farm dog wasn't the right kind of life for Chestnut after all. Maybe the shelter would find him a family and a home where he'd fit in perfectly, where everyone would be as happy as she was to have him.

Meg wrapped her arms around Chestnut's neck and kissed his head. "There's somebody out there that needs you even more than I do," she said into his fur. She steeled herself. It was time.

Meg stood up and carried Chestnut over to the front desk. The woman smiled sympathetically at her.

"Don't you worry, sweetheart," she said to Meg. "A handsome dog like this, he'll have a happy new home in no time. Gosh, he'll probably get adopted right away, since folks like to give dogs as Christmas presents so much. I'll bet he'll be under someone's tree with a bright red bow around his neck by Christmas morning."

Meg tried to force a smile, but it crumbled before it reached the corners of her mouth. Her eyes filled with tears. *Chestnut doesn't belong under anyone else's tree,* she thought. He belonged under hers. He belonged at the end of her bed.

He belonged with her, period.

Chestnut looked at her with such trust as she handed him over to the woman. He didn't mind being held by a stranger, and his tail thwacked against the woman's arm. He kept his gaze on Meg, watching her like they were playing a game and he was waiting for her next move. Chestnut had no reason to think that he and Meg were about to be separated forever. Meg had worked so hard to get him to trust that she would always come back, and that's exactly what he was doing: trusting her. He believed, in a simple, pure way, that she would come back, just like she'd promised.

Meg's heart shattered into a thousand pieces as she watched the woman turn around and carry Chestnut through a metal door at the back of the room. The dog scrambled up onto her shoulder so he could look back at Meg. Even as he moved farther and farther away, his brown eyes stayed on her, never doubting her for an instant. Just as the door swung shut between them, Meg heard him let out one short, sharp whimper of confusion.

Meg turned and ran past her family, through the front door. She made it outside just as the loud, racking sobs burst from her body. She couldn't have stopped them if she'd tried. Ben and Sarah ran after her and started to pull her into a hug, but she shook them off and climbed into the truck. Her family got in, and her dad sat stone-still in the driver's seat for a moment before starting the ignition.

Meg's weeping didn't subside as they began to drive home. Her family exchanged sad glances with each other over her head, but she didn't acknowledge them. She didn't have any room in her heart for anything but her own grief—and her love for Chestnut. What would happen to him? Would the people who adopted him be kind to him? Would they know how much he liked his ears scratched? Would they know to check his paw for infection? Would Chestnut bond with them the way he'd bonded with her, or would he feel lost and confused? Would he miss her for long —or forever?

Meg's mind whirled with questions and regrets. She replayed every decision she'd made since she had found Chestnut, trying to figure out the moment when it had all gone wrong. How had it come to this? What should she have done differently so that he would be here by her side, and not alone in a cage, growing farther in the distance with every passing second?

She didn't deserve a dog like Chestnut. He deserved

to feel safe and happy. She was so angry and disappointed with herself that she felt sick to her stomach.

As the truck turned onto their road, her dad cleared his throat as if to say something, but her mom shook her head and he fell silent again. Ben reached over and squeezed Meg's hand, but she pushed him away. She didn't want his pity. She wanted her dog back. She knew she had been wrong to lie, and wrong to keep Chestnut when she wasn't supposed to. But why wasn't she supposed to?

It all came back to the fact that her mom and dad didn't think she was grown-up enough. They didn't think she was grown-up enough to truly help with the farm. They didn't think she was grown-up enough to take care of a dog. And they didn't think she was grown-up enough to handle losing that dog someday. Meg laughed harshly under her breath. They had tried to protect her from being hurt by getting too attached to a dog, but *they* were the reason she got hurt—not Chestnut. Chestnut hadn't done anything wrong.

Her grief began to turn into something more like

anger. Her parents didn't have to make her get rid of Chestnut.

They could have let her keep him but grounded her from seeing her friends for a month.

Or they could have taken away her screen time.

Or they could have taken back her Christmas presents.

Meg wouldn't have cared what other kind of punishment they had come up with. She would have given back all her Christmas presents past and future if it meant they could have stayed together.

She thought bitterly of her dad. She couldn't believe that he was cruel enough to put Meg and Chestnut through the same heartbreak when he knew how badly it hurt. And her mom's expression when they pulled up to the shelter had been so full of sorrow—and yet she didn't utter a word of protest as they handed Chestnut over to some stranger to be locked in a cage, without a home or a family or someone to love him.

How could they have left him there?

How could her parents do this to her?

★ CHAPTER 18 ★

As soon as the truck came to a stop, Meg hopped out and ran into the house. She stomped up the stairs and flung herself facedown onto her bed, still wearing her coat, scarf, and mittens. She didn't want to talk to anyone, and she didn't want to hear them tell her that she'd move on eventually, that there would be other dogs in her life. She could still smell Chestnut on her mittens, and she pressed them to her face, sobbing quietly until she no longer had even the energy to cry.

Meg was exhausted, and she must have dozed off for a while. She woke suddenly to a dark room and the sound of loud voices carried up from downstairs. She was groggy, confused, and overheated in her winter gear. She rubbed her puffy eyes as she sat up in bed.

Curiosity got the best of her. Meg tiptoed out of her room to the top of the stairs, where she could listen without being seen. She immediately recognized the voice of Mr. Mike, the farm foreman.

"I'm sorry to bother you at suppertime, but it couldn't wait . . ." Mike said, his usually booming and jovial voice sounding distressed.

"It's no bother, Mike. Would you like to stay for supper?" Meg's mom asked. Meg heard her moving around the kitchen rattling pans and opening and closing cupboard doors.

"No, thank you, though I'm sure whatever you're making is delicious. I . . . I have some bad news, guys, and I hate to be the one to tell you all." Mike cleared his throat as if he didn't want to say whatever was about to come next. Meg could picture him, tall and barrel-chested, with his John Deere cap clutched in his hands and his gray hair wispy and mussed.

"What is it, Mike?" her dad asked, his tone serious.

Meg heard the sound of chairs scraping across the floor and boots shuffling on the ground as they all sat down.

"I've just come from the back lots," Mike said. "Somebody . . . Somebody's been chopping there."

"Chopping?" Sarah said. "Our trees?"

"Yes, our trees," Mike said. "Looks like they've . . . run off with about a hundred and fifty of 'em."

"What?" Meg's dad shouted, and she heard him slap the tabletop. "Are you sure?"

"I've never been more sure about anything in my life," Mike said grimly.

Meg's chest tightened. She couldn't believe it. Someone stole their trees? Meg had never heard of anything so awful. It had never occurred to her that someone could break onto their land and steal the only thing keeping her family—and their farm—afloat. They needed those trees.

"Oh my God," Meg's mom gasped.

"Should I call the sheriff, Dad?"

"I'll take care of it," he replied. "Thanks, Sarah."

"I'm sorry to be the bearer of bad news," Mike went

on. "Please let me know what I can do to help." Meg heard a chair scoot back from the table.

"Of course, Mike," her dad said. "You do so much already—thank you for coming to tell us. We'll get through this."

"I know we will."

She could hear Mike leave through the front door. Then she heard her dad murmuring softly, as her mom broke down crying. Meg could almost picture him reassuring her mom that everything would be all right. But it all felt like a lie. It felt like nothing would ever be all right again.

Blood pounded in Meg's ears. This couldn't be real. What kind of person would steal *trees?* It felt like the kind of thing that would happen in a nightmare . . . almost too strange and terrible to believe.

For a second, Meg's anger with her parents about Chestnut got the best of her. *It serves them right for making me get rid of my dog,* she thought. Immediately, though, she felt ashamed. No matter what they had done, she would never wish this on her parents—they couldn't afford the loss of a hundred and fifty trees. They were going to have to lay off workers for sure.

This might even cost them the farm.

Meg felt like she was going to throw up. All of her parents' hard work, all that her brother and sister had done to nurture those trees and run the lot—it was all a waste. Some thief hadn't just taken trees. He had taken everything from them.

Meg wished she were still asleep. She wished she could wake up and Chestnut would still be here. There wouldn't be any stolen trees. Things would be normal again.

But then she heard her dad on the phone calling the sheriff's office. She heard her mom sniffling quietly, and Sarah and Ben trying to comfort her. She knew it wasn't a dream. She sat down at the top of the stairs, shaking and scared.

It was quiet downstairs while the family waited for the sheriff. When Meg heard tires rolling across the gravel driveway, she heard her dad's heavy footsteps moving across the room to open the door.

"I'm sorry to hear about your troubles, Mr. Briggs,"

the woman's voice drifted up to Meg. "Can you tell me what happened?"

Meg's dad recounted what Mr. Mike had told him. She asked several questions, including the value of the trees, when they were last checked, and who else had access to the farm. Then, as they prepared to go out and investigate the scene of the crime, the deputy said, "Listen, Mr. and Mrs. Briggs. I understand that this must be very hard for you. And we all know that trees don't just get up and walk away on their own, which means someone stole them from you. Unfortunately, I . . . Before we go out there, I want to manage your expectations. I don't really know what we'll find or whether we'll be able to track down whoever did this. But even if we found the trees that were stolen, it isn't as if we'll be able to identify them or prove that they're really yours. They're just like any other trees out there, right?"

Meg was practically shaking with anger, because she knew the sheriff was right. The thieves were going to get away with their crime, while her family and the staff of the tree farm were going to suffer.

She heard her mom speaking in a soft tone but couldn't make out the words.

"We'll do what we can, Mrs. Briggs. I promise my team will work as hard as humanly possible to figure out what happened here. But . . . I just want you to be prepared that it's possible nothing will come of our investigation."

Meg's mom and dad left with the sheriff to go to the crime scene while Sarah and Ben finished cooking dinner. Meg had the sudden urge to be downstairs with them. She didn't want to be alone anymore.

When she stepped into the kitchen, Sarah stopped stirring the pasta and looked at Meg with a concerned expression. "Did you hear?"

Meg nodded, but her emotions were too close to the surface for her to speak. Ben looked equal parts furious and worried, but when his eyes met Meg's he put down his spatula and wrapped her in a hug. "It's going to be all right. Mom and Dad will figure something out. Don't worry, Micro."

Meg pulled away and looked him square in the eye. "Stop telling me not to worry, Ben!"

"I'm sorry—" He shook his head, as if to scold himself.

"Meg," Sarah started to say. "Ben didn't mean—"

"Stop!" Meg said. "Both of you, stop treating me like I'm some little baby you have to protect. We're all part of the same family. We're all worried about the same things. I'm not too young to understand how bad things are for our family right now. I told you that earlier, Ben!"

Ben looked at the floor, and Sarah studied her sister's face intently.

"You're right," Ben said.

"You are," Sarah said. "You're right that things are really bad and that we shouldn't treat you like this. I'm sorry, Meg. I just hate seeing you so upset. You're my little sister—I used to change your diapers."

Meg screwed up her face. "Ew."

"Trust me, it was grosser for me." Sarah lightly punched Meg on the arm. "I can't help it. I just don't want you to be scared."

"Ditto." Ben sighed.

Meg pushed up the sleeves of her flannel shirt.

"I forgive you," she said, then added, "What can I do?"

Ben ruffled her hair and handed her a head of broccoli. "Start there," he said, as he flipped over the chicken breasts sizzling in the pan.

Their parents returned from the lot, and Meg heard the deputy's car pull out of the driveway. The five of them ate in silence, the day's events weighing heavily on all of them. Meg's mom's eyes were red and raw as she sniffled throughout the meal. Her dad stared off angrily into space, his rigatoni with chicken and broccoli getting cold on his plate. Meg watched her family, the worry so thick in the room it felt like she could reach out and touch it.

A startling thought began to take shape in Meg's head, and in an instant she knew that there was one way to solve this mystery. But her parents had made her drop the only creature who could make that happen at the animal shelter. Better still, Chestnut could have prevented this from happening in the first place. He wouldn't have let those thieves onto their property.

He would have sensed their presence, alerted the farm staff, and driven them away. But now that the trees were gone, what better way to track them down than with an expert tracking dog?

Now Meg didn't just miss her dog—she needed him, too.

Meg's mind was a jumble of ideas and feelings as she picked at her dinner. She knew without a doubt that Chestnut would be able to help find the stolen trees. She looked at her mom and dad, at their strained faces and empty stares. If they knew what she was thinking, they'd be more than disappointed or angry. They'd be furious. But it was a chance Meg was willing to take. She was going to have to do something drastic, maybe even a little crazy. She could get into a lifetime of trouble, but it was worth the risk. She would do anything for her family.

She needed to get her dog back. First she'd have to figure out exactly how to do it.

★ CHAPTER 19 ★

After dinner was finished and the kitchen was cleaned up, Meg's mom and dad went upstairs to their bedroom. They said they were going to turn in early, but when Meg went up to her bedroom, she could hear them talking through their door. She was glad she couldn't hear what they were saying. A part of her knew that the theft of the trees had distracted them from fully administering her punishment, but she didn't care anymore. She had bigger things on her mind.

Meg went back downstairs and peeked into the living room. Sarah sat on the couch with her phone. Meg assumed she was texting her friends. Ben was curled up in the recliner with a book, but Meg didn't think he was really reading. His eyes were stuck on the same spot on the page, and his mind seemed far away. Without saying anything, Meg headed past the living room, through the kitchen, and into the mudroom. She pulled on her boots and coat, hat and scarf, and slipped outside. She was prepared to say that she was just going out for a walk to clear her head, but nobody saw her leave, let alone asked where she was going. They were all too upset themselves.

As soon as she was outside, she ran to the barn and got her bike. The air was biting and clear as night settled over the mountain, and Meg shivered even in her thick new coat. She closed the barn door and hopped on her bike, pedaling quickly toward Colton's house. She needed him in order for her plan to succeed. If he agreed to help her out, she knew that she would owe him big time.

She skidded into Colton's driveway and let her bike fall to the ground. She raced up the porch steps and knocked on the screen door that led into the Johnsons' mudroom. The dogs were all curled on the floor just inside, and as she approached, they jumped up, barking excitedly in greeting. After a long moment, Colton's mom, Dr. Shirley, came to the door.

"Well, hello, Meg. How are you, tonight?" Dr. Shirley asked, wiping her hands on a dishtowel as she opened the door for Meg.

"I'm fine, thanks, Dr. Shirley," Meg said. "How are you?"

"I'm whooped," Shirley said with a smile. "I spent all afternoon over on the Stevens' farm vaccinating their new litter of puppies." She chuckled. "Wrangling thirteen black Lab pups is harder than trying to teach them the alphabet."

"That sounds hard." Meg smiled, trying her best to seem pleasant and normal. "I'm sorry to come over so late. Is Colton home? I need to ask him a favor."

"Of course, of course," Dr. Shirley said. "He's inside playing a game of chess with his dad. Do you want to come in?"

Meg nodded and followed Dr. Shirley inside. Colton was sitting at the kitchen table with his dad, Dr. Marcus, and from the looks of things, Dr. Marcus was just about to win the whole game.

"Ugh," Colton groaned as his dad took his last bishop. "I was trying to get closer to your queen."

"Yeah, but you've always got to keep an eye on the rooks behind you, kiddo." Dr. Marcus was a tall, broad-shouldered man with smile lines around his eyes. Meg thought Colton was going to look just like his dad when he grew up.

"Good evening, Megan," Dr. Marcus said, glancing at her quickly before turning his attention back to the game. "How are things over at the tree farm?" He always called her Megan, no matter how many times Colton told him to call her Meg.

Meg shrugged, unsure at first whether she should tell them about the stolen trees. "I guess they could be better," she finally said.

Dr. Marcus looked back up at her. "Everything all right?" His voice was full of genuine concern.

"Oh, it's just been a rough day," Meg said, hoping she sounded less shaky than she felt.

Dr. Marcus nodded knowingly. "I'm sorry to hear that, but I do understand. Some days are harder than others." He sighed. "When you run your own business, it's a lot of responsibility, and it's all on you. Shirley and I get it."

"We do," Shirley piped in.

Meg knew that Colton's parents were large-animal veterinarians. They drove around taking care of the horses, cattle, pigs, and sheep—as well as the occasional litter of puppies—on area farms. Colton had told her once about a disease that swept through the cattle farms of the county. His parents had worked day and night to try to save them but had lost more cows than they'd saved. Meg couldn't imagine how hard that must have been on Dr. Marcus and Dr. Shirley and the farmers. She supposed they probably did know how it felt to be helpless.

Meg slid into the chair next to Colton and tried to be patient while they finished their game. After a few minutes and a few more moves, Dr. Marcus said, "Checkmate."

Colton sighed, then held out his hand to shake his dad's. "Good game, Dad."

Dr. Marcus pumped his son's hand up and down. "Good game, kid."

Colton looked at Meg. "You want to go downstairs?"

Meg nodded and they escaped down the stairs to Colton's finished basement, which was equipped with a large couch, a big-screen television, and all of Colton's baseball paraphernalia.

"What's up?" Colton asked as he flopped onto the couch and grabbed the remote.

Meg sat down beside him. Usually she kicked off her shoes and settled into the fluffy cushions, but this time she sat upright on the edge of the sofa, too tense to even lean back.

"I need your help," she said without preamble. Colton raised a questioning eyebrow, and she continued. "Chestnut got out today and came to the house. I . . . I ended up confessing everything, and my mom and dad made me take him to the shelter." Her voice trembled, but she forced back the tears. She didn't have time for crying right now.

"Oh, shoot," Colton said. "I'm really sorry."

She was so grateful for her friend in that moment. He didn't say "I told you so," and he didn't tell her that everything would work out. He just sympathized with her. Colton was always so good at saying the right thing.

She bit her lip, then continued. "It was awful. I feel so guilty for lying to my parents. And to Chestnut. I told him I'd never leave him, but I was wrong, and I had to hand him over to a stranger. You should have seen his face . . ." Meg felt a sharp pang in her chest and couldn't finish the sentence.

Colton nodded. "What do you need my help with?"

Meg looked down at her hands, then back up at him. Everything was riding on Colton saying yes. She took a breath and knew that she had to come right out with it.

"Somebody robbed the tree farm, Colt."

"What—when?"

"Today. They cut down a bunch of trees and took them. Things were already really tight this year, and now . . . now we might even have to let some of the staff go." This time, she couldn't hold back her tears. "I don't know what's going to happen, but . . ." Meg was quiet for a second, waiting until she could speak without sobbing. "But I know Chestnut could find our trees and whoever did this. He can track them and send those dumb thieves to jail and that would really help the farm and maybe . . . maybe my mom and dad would let me keep him after all." She finished and felt totally drained.

Colton looked at her with wide eyes and shook his head, as if he was still processing everything she had said. "Who would steal Christmas trees? That's like the least Christmas-y move ever—what a grinch."

Meg nodded. It was hard to imagine that someone cared so little about Christmas or the holiday spirit —let alone other people—that they could do such a cruel thing. And she hated the thought that strangers had snuck around her farm without anyone knowing.

"I know I kept a lot of secrets and lied to everyone. Even you," Meg said. "You don't have to forgive me —but will you help me?"

Colton didn't even hesitate. "Of course," he said.

For the millionth time, Meg told herself she had the best best friend ever.

"What do you need me to do?"

"Come with me to the shelter and tell them that

you and your parents are going to foster Chestnut," Meg began. "I mean, you guys have so many dogs around here that your folks probably won't even notice another one, right?"

Colton rolled his eyes. "That's ridiculous, Meg. Of course they'll notice."

Despite the circumstances, Meg couldn't help but chuckle at the look on his face. "I was kidding about that part. But I really do think I can actually fix everything, once and for all."

"Okay," he said. He looked her right in the eye. "This is crazy. You know that, right, Meg?"

"Yup."

He laughed. "Well, as long as we're in agreement then. Give me a minute or two to convince my mom and dad."

★ CHAPTER 20 ★

Meg stayed downstairs while Colton went up to sweet-talk his parents. He came back down just a few minutes later. "Okay," he said, glancing back over his shoulder. "I only told them the basics—that you found a dog and are trying to convince your parents to keep him. They agreed to foster him for a few days." He shot Meg a serious look. "I left out the whole part about Chestnut helping you track down criminals, since they're definitely not going to go for that. I don't suppose I can talk you out of that, can I?"

Meg jumped up and ran over to him. "Thank you!" she said, throwing her arms around him in a big, grateful hug. "And no, definitely not."

"Yeah, I figured you weren't going to give up that easily," Colton said, hugging her back. "But at least I can say I tried. Now let's go get your dog before anything else crazy happens. Or before I change my mind."

Upstairs, Dr. Shirley gave Colton a handwritten note on her official veterinary practice letterhead, with her signature at the bottom. "This tells Janice at the shelter that we're okay with you bringing Chestnut here." She looked at Meg. "Meg, I need you to understand that this is only a temporary fix, okay? We can't keep him here forever."

Meg nodded enthusiastically. "I understand, Dr. Shirley. I promise. Thank you so, so much."

Dr. Shirley gave her a hug. "I know how it feels to fall in love with your first dog." She smiled nostalgically, then jerked a thumb toward the sleepy pack curled up together on the mudroom floor. "And your hundredth." She clapped her hands together. "Okay, team. Reflector vests and helmets—both of you—and watch for ice."

In the mudroom, Colton stepped over and around

snorting dogs and layered on his winter gear. He handed Meg a neon yellow vest with shiny strips of reflector tape all over it. "Mom's rules," he said before pulling one over his own coat. He shoved a spare collar and leash into his coat pocket.

Meg put the vest on over her purple coat and followed him outside into the dark.

The ride into town took them about twenty minutes. By the time the shelter's sign came into view, Meg's legs were buzzing from exertion, but she was filled with hope. Chestnut was waiting for her, and she was going to bring him home.

They parked their bikes and ran inside just as the shelter volunteer was turning off the lights. "Hey Colton," the woman said. She nodded at Meg, whom she'd just met earlier that evening. "Hi, sweetheart. Good to see you again. But we're closed for the night, kids. You'll have to come back tomorrow."

"Oh please—I can't!" Meg cried. Her knees felt weak with fear that she'd missed her chance by moments. "We have to get Chestnut tonight." She didn't want to cry in front of the woman twice in one day, but she could feel the sting of fresh tears building behind her eyes.

"Please, Janice," Colton said, pulling the piece of paper out of his pocket. He handed it to the volunteer. "This is from my mom. She gave me permission to foster the Plott hound that the Briggs family brought in earlier."

Janice's face fell and she looked at them with genuine pity in her eyes. "Oh, kids, I'm so sorry." She shook her head slowly. "That dog was adopted an hour ago."

"What?" Meg cried out. The dam broke and fat tears streamed down her face, but she didn't care anymore. What was left of her heart had broken all over again.

Colton put a protective arm around her, and she buried her face on his shoulder to cry. "It's okay, Meg." He turned back to Janice. "The Plott hound—he's brindled—brown and black?"

"That's the one," she said.

"And you're sure he was adopted and not fostered?"

Colton continued. "Maybe they were just going to take him home for a little while?"

"No, sorry." Janice shook her head again. "It was a family, and they were pretty excited about finding the exact dog they'd been wanting. They'd come by here a few times in the last few weeks but never quite connected with the right dog. Until they saw the Plott." She smiled at the memory. "And the little boy was just so excited—he said he's been waiting for a dog with four white paws."

"Wait—what?" Meg's head popped up. "Did you say four white paws?"

"Yes, hon. Four white paws. Just like the dog you brought in today."

"Chestnut only has one white paw!" Meg said, her voice high and excited. "Colton—it wasn't him!"

Colton smiled cautiously. "Can we just check to see if her dog is still here?"

Janice started to shake her head.

"Please?" Meg said. "It's so important—we need Chestnut to help my family."

"I—" The woman started to speak, but then seemed to change her mind. "Sure. You two are very sweet, and you"—she tipped her head at Meg—"really seem like you've had a rough day. Why not."

She led them through the door at the back of the room. As soon as they stepped through it, a chaotic chorus of barks rang out at the far end of a long hallway.

They turned a corner at the end of the hall and came to a stop in a massive room lined with rows of kennels stacked three high. Meg tried to listen for Chestnut's familiar bark, but she couldn't pick it out with all the other dogs barking too. Meg ran down one row, then another, scanning every cage frantically.

"Do you see him?" she called out to Colton, who was searching the next row over.

"No," he shouted back.

Meg turned down the last row, worry creeping in that she wouldn't find him after all. Then, at last, Meg heard one bark rise above all the others. It was heartbreakingly familiar, and Meg sucked in her breath.

"It's him!" she cried to Colton. "Chestnut—is that you?"

At the end of the row she froze, her eyes locked on the most magnificent sight she had ever seen. Chestnut was in the middle kennel, paws up on the door, his nose pressed through the metal wire. He was shaking and barking and whining, clearly overwhelmed by all the sights, sounds, and smells. At the sight of her, he instantly started wagging his tail and wriggling around the cage like crazy.

"Hi, buddy," she said as calmly as she could, trying to soothe him. "Shhhh . . . it's okay—I'm here now. You're okay." She unlatched the door and it opened with a squeak.

Colton rounded the corner just as Chestnut was hurtling himself out of the kennel and into Meg's arms. She laughed as the dog squirmed and covered her face in sloppy dog kisses and squirmed some more.

Janice came up behind them. "I have never been more glad to be wrong in my entire life," she laughed. "Someone's happy to see you."

"Not as happy as I am to see him," Meg said, feeling like she might actually burst with happiness. She put the dog down on the ground and wiped away the last of her tears with her sleeve. "Can we take him home, ma'am?"

Chestnut spun in a circle, doing a goofy, happy dance. He barked playfully at Janice, then sat down right at her feet, gazing up at her with big, pleading eyes. They all laughed, and Janice bent down and scratched Chestnut behind the ears.

"I'm not sure I could stop you if I tried," she said, grinning up at Meg. "Look at this face!" She patted Chestnut, who looked from her to Meg and back again. "Yes," Janice said. "You can take him home where he belongs."

Colton signed the forms while Meg slipped the collar over Chestnut's head and snapped the leash onto it. "I'm so sorry you had to come here, buddy," Meg whispered into his ear. "And I'm sorry for scaring you, but I have a new plan, and if it works, we're going to be together after all. First we've got a job to do though."

Chestnut blinked at her patiently, as if he understood what she was saying. Meg clicked her tongue and he followed her out the door, ready to get to work.

★ CHAPTER 21 ★

Chestnut ran cheerfully beside Meg's bike the whole way back to Colton's. Meg kept looking at him out of the corner of her eye, unable to really believe that she had him back. She wasn't sure how she would repay Colton for all of his help, but she knew she'd have to do something amazing for him and his family. Without them, Chestnut would still be stuck in a cage in that cold, lonely shelter.

When she thought about him there, her anger at her parents flared up. She wasn't being fair, she knew. They were just being parents, and she was the one who had lied in the first place. She'd gotten herself into some serious trouble, but still . . . it seemed so cruel that they had forced her to abandon Chestnut.

But Meg had a more pressing issue to worry about right then: figuring out who had stolen their trees. She knew she'd have to forgive her parents eventually. Maybe when she and Chestnut solved the crime, they'd be able to forgive her, too. As they stopped at the end of Colton's driveway, she turned her thoughts to how they would get started.

"I'm just going to take Chestnut over to the spot where the trees were taken," she said. "And then I'll bring him back here, okay?"

"Sure," Colton said. "I promised Dad a rematch, so I'd better get in there. When you bring him back, I'll introduce him to my parents and get him settled."

Meg handed him her reflector vest, then reached out her gloved fist, and Colton bumped it with his. "Thanks, Colt," she said. "For everything."

Colton nodded. "That's what friends are for." He rode up the driveway. Just before he pulled his bike into the barn, he turned back. "Be careful, Meg the Leg."

"Always," Meg replied.

She rode back toward her family's property and ditched her bike outside the fence line between Colton's land and hers. Now that she and Chestnut were out on their own, at night, far from any houses, she was starting to get a little nervous. She'd never been afraid on her own farm before, but no one had ever stolen anything there either.

The quickest route to the spot where the trees were cut down was across the fields. "Come on, boy," Meg said to Chestnut as she ducked between the fence rails. He hopped through them right behind her. "Let's go solve a mystery," she said to her dog.

Chestnut seemed happy to follow wherever she led him. When they got to the back lot where the trees had been cut down, Meg gasped. Just as Mr. Mike had said, someone had come along and cut down every single tree in this corner of the farm, leaving only short stumps behind. Though she knew what had happened, seeing the proof of it felt like a punch in the gut. This was more than a theft. This was a violation of her family's safety too.

It was so upsetting that Meg couldn't afford to think about it right then. From what she could make out, the ground was covered with fresh snow and speckled with the pine needles and pinecones that covered every acre of the tree farm. She didn't see any footprints — which meant the snow had fallen *after* the trees had been cut down. That could be important information.

Here and there Meg saw a depression under the snow, which, she thought, looked a little like a spot where a tree had been dragged. She stood still and scanned the area, carefully observing every detail she could make out in the beam of her flashlight, sorting out which ones could be clues. She didn't see anything obvious, so it was time to put Chestnut to work.

She signaled to him with a click of her tongue. He ran to her, and she dipped her fingers in some sap dripping off one of the tree stumps. She held the sap out to him, and he sniffed and snorted, inhaled and exhaled, absorbing every detail about the trees that he could. When he was ready, she gave him the command.

"Chestnut, go find it!"

Chestnut instantly got to work. He skimmed his

nose along the ground, leaving little marks in the snow. He was following an invisible path, stopping at each stump for an instant before moving on to the next. At the end of a row, he moved farther along and turned right, walking along the fence. Meg ran to catch up with him. "What is it—did you find something?"

Chestnut had sped up into a trot. Meg could see that he was in the zone, just like he had been when he'd first hunted pinecones. This part of the farm was ringed in chain link. The dog ran along the fence line for a few yards until he came to a sudden stop. He pawed at the ground, sniffed at the snow, and bobbed his head around the metal wire, his nostrils twitching furiously.

Meg held her breath as she watched and waited. Finally, Chestnut raised his snout to scent the air, then looked at Meg and barked excitedly.

He had found something!

She ran over to his side and saw, right in front of him, a torn shred of dark fabric snagged on a jagged point of metal. The fence had been clipped in several places and pried open, making a hole big enough for a full-grown person to climb through. This was where the thieves had entered the farm, Meg realized. That meant this scrap of fabric had to be from something one of the robbers was wearing. The thought made her shudder.

Chestnut pressed his nose to the fabric as if to make sure she saw it, then barked again and clambered through the fence. Meg snatched the piece of cloth and stuffed it in her coat pocket, then followed Chestnut through the opening, careful not to scratch herself on the sharp ends. Chestnut shot off into the woods surrounding the farm. He was on the case.

Meg ran after him, blood pounding in her ears.

As she followed her dog through the dark forest, she imagined a world where they were the heroes of Briggs Family Tree Farm. She could see her dad smiling proudly as he explained to the staff that thanks to Meg and Chestnut, not only would they get to keep their jobs, but they'd be getting a Christmas bonus, too. She imagined Mr. Mike patting her on the shoulder with gratitude. The others would cheer and give Chestnut happy scratches behind the ears. Sarah and

Ben would wink at her as they applauded. And her mom would come over with a perfectly sized doggy Christmas sweater that she'd slip over Chestnut's head and around his paws. When Meg would look at it, she'd see it said "Briggs" on it—and she'd know Chestnut was hers forever.

Meg smiled to herself as this wonderful scene played in her mind. But as she watched Chestnut beeline toward their target, she knew that he had no worries about what Meg's family would say. He wasn't focused on saving anything. His only concern was to follow his training, and that meant tracking the scent that he had found. Meg was a little bit jealous—she wished that she could forget everything else that was bubbling and roiling through her mind.

They climbed over a fallen log and for a moment, Chestnut stopped. He seemed to be staring off into the distance, not particularly focused on anything. Panic shot through Meg. What if he'd lost the trail?

She saw that his nose was twitching. He swung his head from side to side, then sniffed some more. He took two steps in one direction, then three in another.

Finally, after a moment that felt like a lifetime to Meg, Chestnut barked. He spun around, ran back to the log, and sniffed underneath and all around it until he picked up a scent again. This time, he headed off at a sharp angle, and Meg saw a new bounce in his step —a renewed excitement as he followed the scent, his training, and his instincts.

Meg was in awe of her dog. He was adorable, he was sweet, and he was a good boy. And on top of all that, he was an amazing tracker who did things no human—nor even most dogs—could do. She wished she had thought to bring some treats, because Chestnut deserved a reward for all of his hard work.

Chestnut was moving faster and faster. Meg wondered how far they would have to go to find the trees, but it didn't matter. She would go as far as she needed to, and she knew Chestnut was just as dedicated. His nose would lead them to the truth.

They headed deeper into the woods, hot on the trail of the thieves who were trying to ruin their family Christmas.

★ CHAPTER 22 ★

Though the trees were thick, the moon was high. As Chestnut led Meg deeper into the woods, it lit their way. Every few minutes, Chestnut got so far ahead of her that she couldn't see him, but when she whistled or called his name he stopped. His tail wagged while he waited for her, but she could tell that he was impatient. As soon as he decided she was close enough, he turned and dashed forward again, his nose leading him onward.

After they'd trekked for a while, the moon slipped behind a cloud, the woods went dark, and suddenly Meg could barely see three feet in front of her. But she wasn't afraid. She'd spent her entire childhood traipsing through these woods, exploring and pretending. She just didn't want to get separated from Chestnut.

"Chestnut," she called. "To me." She'd heard Colton say this to his dogs many times, and she hoped it would work.

Immediately, she heard the dog's footsteps heading back toward her. She knelt down and waited for him, then scratched his head and snuggled him when he got there. "You're such a good boy, Chestnut," she said. "I can't see as well as you can. Can you stay close?"

As if he understood, Chestnut slowed down while Meg picked up her pace, and together they closed the distance between them. Hopping over fallen trees, scrambling through rock-littered gullies, Meg followed Chestnut. The dog was like a tracking machine. Occasionally he stopped, lifting his nose from the ground to sniff at the air before darting off to follow the scent again.

Time slipped by, and Meg shivered as the night grew colder. A lot colder. Every time she inhaled she felt the icy air way down deep in her lungs. The farther she got from the farm, the more undisturbed the land was—and the deeper the snow on the ground. Her legs sank shin-deep, making it harder and harder to walk.

Meg squinted into the darkness, broken every couple minutes by a flash of moonlight, and realized that they'd gone deeper into the forest than she'd ever been before. She'd been so focused on following Chestnut that she'd lost track of the direction they were heading, and now she was disoriented. Which direction was the farm? Where was the lot, or Colton's house? The land, the trees—even the air felt different and unfamiliar wherever they were.

"Chestnut, stop," she called out. He stood still, one paw frozen midstep, and turned back to look at her expectantly. "Hold on, buddy," she said. She felt a tiny wriggle of fear. Even if she and Chestnut could find the stolen trees, what if they couldn't find their way home again? She needed to get her bearings.

Meg scanned the immediate area and spotted a clearing up ahead. It was a good place to stop and plant herself while she tried to spot a landmark or plot their location. "Come on, Chestnut," she said. "Let's figure out where we are."

The clouds cracked open, and the moon beamed down from high above them. Snow crunched beneath her boots. With Chestnut trotting close at her side, Meg reached the open area and looked up at the stars, trying to spot the North Star. She wasn't an expert, but she figured she could do that much.

As Chestnut wandered a few feet away to trace a scent, Meg spun in a slow circle, her eyes locked on the sky. Suddenly the snow shifted beneath her feet. Just as Chestnut let out a loud, sharp bark of alarm and warning, Meg screamed.

In the space of a single breath, the ground beneath her gave way. She was submerged in an icy pond so cold that it felt like her whole body was being squeezed in a horrible monster's grip. Meg flailed wildly, and frigid water filled her mouth and nose and splashed in her eyes. She couldn't see anything around her. She was chin deep, and her hair was soaked. She had no thoughts, no ideas, no words—there was only the crushing pain of the bitterly cold water.

Then, somehow, through the blank of her mind, Meg heard a soft, distant sound. At first, she couldn't make it out—couldn't understand what it was. It was rhythmic, repetitive—a single sound playing over and over and over again until it sounded like one. It was loud and insistent. It tugged at her mind, demanding her attention more than the pain or fear or cold. Meg focused on the sound. Somehow, she understood that she needed to move toward it, so she kicked upward. Her waterlogged boots and coat felt like they weighed a hundred pounds each, and her limbs were weak. Where had all her strength gone? But she pushed herself on. Whatever that sound was, she had to get to it.

Her shoulder knocked into something hard and cold. The layer of ice that covered the pond. Though her limbs were almost entirely numb, she raised her arms out of the water and tried to pull herself up onto the ice. She lifted her head and there was Chestnut, standing above her, barking frantically. Barking. That was the sound she had heard. Chestnut.

Meg coughed, spitting out water as she gasped for air. She tried to catch hold of something, but her wet gloves were too slippery and the surface of the ice was too slick for her to grab onto. The ice began to crumble at her touch, falling away under her as she flailed her arms desperately. With a heart-rending howl, Chestnut leaped forward and snapped at her sleeve, grabbing it with his front teeth. He held on with all his power, but the unsteady layer beneath him gave way too. His front paws slipped into the freezing water, and he yelped in pain—but held tightly to Meg's jacket.

Meg sank lower in the water. Her eyes began to close, and she didn't have much strength left to fight her way back up. She felt a powerful pulling on her arm though, and it was keeping her from going under. She opened her eyes just in time to see Chestnut again, this time sliding downward toward her, scrambling with his hind legs to pull himself backwards. She realized with horror that she was pulling him under with her. Adrenaline shot through Meg's body like lightning, and her mind snapped back into focus. *No!*

As if an unseen force was raising her up from below, Meg gripped at the ice with her gloved hands and managed to lift her shoulders out of the water.

She heaved Chestnut backwards with one hand. He couldn't help but let go of her coat as he scuttled onto safer ground. He began barking again frantically, desperately, intensely.

Meg finally got a better grip on the ice, and she tried to pull herself farther up, but it was so hard. All of her strength had been sapped by the cold. She clawed at the cold surface, straining to hang on. Just as she thought she couldn't make it another second, she felt something warm and soft against her cheek. Chestnut was there, his face close to hers, giving her his strength. She grabbed hold of his collar, her frozen fingers stiff and unbending. He barked a warning before pulling backwards, his claws scratching and sliding as he tried to dig into the ice. She held on with every last drop of hope she had.

Chestnut pulled harder, giving her just the tiniest bit of leverage she needed to hinge herself up and out of the water, onto the ice. Meg whimpered as she kicked and pulled and slid on her belly to safer ground. The winter air felt warm compared to the water, and her whole body felt like it was on fire as her nerves came back to life. Her chest ached and burned like it was going to explode. But Chestnut was there, at her side, nudging at her and misting her face with his warm breath. When she finally reached a firm spot on the snow-covered dirt, she rolled over onto her back, and he hovered over her, as if he were checking her for injury.

"Chestnut," she gasped, reaching up and pulling him in close. "You saved me. You saved my life." She couldn't keep from crying, and as the hot tears streamed down her face, she let out a long, hoarse sob. Chestnut looked so upset that Meg only cried harder, and she was pretty sure he would have too if he could have. He studied her face questioningly, helplessly, then howled plaintively. He stopped only long enough to lick her tears before howling once more.

"I'm okay, buddy," she choked out. "Thanks to you." She couldn't believe how close she'd come to disaster, and how thankful she was for her dog. "I'm okay," she repeated, as much for herself as for Chestnut.

He lay down next to her, warming her with his body. Meg huddled with him while her heart rate slowed and she began to breathe more evenly. After a few minutes, Chestnut licked her face gently one last time, then stood up. He looked at her, then sniffed at the air. He pawed at the ground, then sniffed at it. He held her gaze again, and this time there was a message in his eyes.

Get up, Chestnut seemed to be telling her. He whimpered at her and put one paw on her shoulder. With a wince, Meg rolled onto her side and pushed herself to a seated position, then slowly stood and shook out her arms and legs. She knew he was right. She had to move—she couldn't just lie there or she'd freeze to death.

And they still had a job to do.

Meg took a few halting steps as her legs came back to life. Water squished out of her boots, and water dripped from her clothes onto the ground. She didn't know how she'd ever be warm again. Chestnut barked, then scented the air once more.

Meg's whole body was stiff, but moving helped warm her up. With every step, she hoped that they were getting closer and closer to the stolen trees. They had come too far to turn back now.

★ CHAPTER 23 ★

Meg struggled to lift one foot. Then the other. She and Chestnut had an important mission, but it was getting harder to stay focused on it with every painful step. She was exhausted. She shivered in her wet clothes and her jeans were stiff, as if they'd started to freeze right onto her body. The moon had reached a high point above them. It was getting late.

This had been a terrible mistake. Meg wanted badly to turn back, but one thought kept her moving forward: she wasn't going to disappoint her family, and she wasn't going to disappoint Chestnut. She couldn't take back the lies she had told them, but she knew she could get the trees back. *Chestnut* could get them back.

She followed the dog down the steep, rough side of another gully. Her boots slipped on the slick snow and she stumbled. She windmilled her arms and almost managed to stay upright . . . until her feet flew out from under her and she fell down with a loud thump, which knocked the wind out of her. Meg lay in the snow for a second, hard rocks poking her in the back, wishing she could just stay there for a little while longer. Chestnut ran back to her and swiped at her with one paw.

"Just give me a second?" She sounded like she was asking her mom for five more minutes of sleep. But Chestnut was having none of it. He nudged her with his snout and let out a high-pitched yip, as if to scold her into getting up.

"Easy for you to say." Meg groaned. It was harder than ever to push herself back up, but she did it. Chestnut waited for her, eyeing her curiously as she eased herself to a standing position.

They made their way to the top of the gully, and he stayed close to her side, keeping a watchful eye on her. Meg plodded heavily through the snow. Her toes and fingers ached and shoots of pain pricked at her skin like hot needles.

As they stepped onto level ground, Chestnut's behavior suddenly changed. He had been focused before, but mostly it was his nose that had been working hard. Now all his senses and his entire body were engaged. Though he stood stock-still, every muscle was flexed and ready to leap into motion. His ears were tuned to a frequency Meg couldn't hear. His fur twitched and flicked as a cold breeze brushed against him. He licked his lips, as if tasting the air.

Meg stood still and observed him, waiting for a sign of what he would do next. His tail stuck straight up in the air. He crouched down and began creeping forward steadily, his head down as if he were stalking his prey. There was nothing of the silly, excitable pup in him now. He was on the job.

Meg could only hope that meant they were getting closer to the end of this journey—and to whoever left the scrap of shirt. The thought that they might be near the people who had stolen their trees made Meg shudder. She pulled her coat tighter around herself, and not because she thought it would keep her warm. Just then, something wet and cold brushed against her cheek, and she buried her face in her frozen mittens and shook her head. It was snowing. Just what they needed.

Meg looked up to find snowflakes swirling in the air all around them. Clouds passed in front of the moon, which cast a spooky, silvery light over the woods.

"C-come on, Meg," she stammered to herself. "P-push harder. You can do this." She picked up her pace, despite her cold, aching feet and her uncontrollable shivering.

Beside her, Chestnut growled low in his throat. A ridge of fur stood up along his spine, which made the hair on Meg's neck stand on end too. Suddenly the dog bolted forward, his eyes on something she couldn't make out in the darkness. Meg stumbled to keep up with him, her insides churning. Chestnut dashed between two trees and for an instant, Meg lost sight of him. She pushed her way after him, snagging her pant leg on a branch that dug into her skin painfully.

Chestnut leaped over a fallen log, then stopped. He dropped his head down and his nose skimmed the snow. Meg watched, breathing heavily, as he searched for the scent he was after. He followed his nose and moved in a tight circle, leaving pawprints in the snow.

With a whimper, he raised his head to sniff at the air. Meg realized that he had lost the trail, and her heart sank. They were so close—how could this happen? Desperation threatened to wash over her.

Then, almost as quickly as he'd lost the scent, Chestnut picked it up again. He homed in on it and dashed off to his left. Meg sloshed in the snow, struggling to keep up. This time, Chestnut wasn't going to wait for her. He didn't look back, and Meg worried that she'd lose sight of him completely now.

Pale moonlight illuminated the tracks that Chestnut had left in the snow, but the large snowflakes hurtling toward the ground threatened to cover them quickly. Meg followed the paw prints as fast as she could, forcing herself to keep going despite the heaviness of her legs. She was so tired. Her mind was begging for sleep, and her body seemed quite willing to give in to its demands. She could neither hear him nor see him, but she believed in her heart that he wouldn't abandon her, just like she would never abandon him.

She grunted with every step after grueling step and tried to remember all the reasons why she was out in the freezing cold, hunting for thieves. She pictured her mom and dad, proud and happy that she'd saved the day. She pictured Mr. Mike and his family, grateful that she'd saved his job. She pictured Ben and Sarah, hugging her—and Chestnut. But most of all, she imagined Chestnut curled up at the foot of her bed. She would keep him warm and safe, and he'd know that they'd never be apart again.

As the image of Chestnut in her room filled her mind, she began to feel warmer. Her teeth stopped chattering. Through the trees, she caught a glimpse of brindled fur and a wagging tail, and she hurried to catch up to her dog. She smiled at the thought of warm quilts and doggy breath. This was what she was pushing toward. This was the thing she wanted most in all the world.

★ CHAPTER 24 ★

Without warning, Meg and Chestnut burst out of the woods into a small field. In the center was a log house, its windows brightly lit behind the curtains. Smoke twisted out of the chimney, and Meg heard laughter from inside the house. Her heart thudded in her chest. The home looked so warm and inviting, for a moment she almost considered knocking on the door.

The spell was broken by the sound of a soft growl. She looked down to find Chestnut standing next to her, his eyes locked on the house and his fur standing on end again. His stance reminded her why they were there: this was where the trail led. Those laughing voices belonged to the people who had stolen her family's trees. The cozy cabin was a den of thieves.

Chestnut began scenting the edge of the yard, close to the tree line. Meg ducked down and hustled after him, afraid that the moonlight would make her visible to the cabin's inhabitants. Another laugh rang out from inside the house, then Meg heard the cabin door open. She lunged behind the nearest tree, pulling Chestnut with her by his furry scruff. A man stepped out onto the porch and cleared his throat. She couldn't get a very good look at him, but she could see the bright light of a cellphone screen in his hand.

"Yeah, it's me," he said, pressing the phone to his ear. "It's done. We've got them."

Meg's heart pounded so hard she thought for sure he would hear it.

"Tomorrow morning? What time?" the man asked.

Silence hung over the yard for a long moment. "Yes, sir," the man finally said. "We'll deliver them at ten o'clock. I know the place." He paused, listening. "Yes, sir. Twenty dollars each. Just like we discussed."

He hung up. Meg could see him staring off into

the distance, as though he were thinking hard about something. A low growl escaped Chestnut's throat. Meg pressed a hand to his back, silently urging him to stay quiet. The man on the porch scanned the field and the edge of the woods—his eyes mercifully missing Meg and Chestnut. His gaze rested on a driveway off to their left for a long moment, then he turned and went back inside.

After Meg heard the cabin door close, she counted to fifty before moving. Chestnut stayed still too, as if he understood what was at stake. Finally, she released his collar. "Come on, boy," she whispered. "Go find those trees."

Chestnut took off to their left, heading for the driveway that the man had been staring at. She followed after him, trying to move quietly through the snow. Her gaze flicked to the cabin door. What if someone came out again? She and Chestnut were totally visible in the clearing. What if they had guns? What if they were worse than thieves?

Chestnut seemed to know exactly where he was headed now. She could see from his unwavering direction that he'd found what he was looking for. As they stepped onto the driveway and began running along its length, Meg spotted a hulking, motionless mass in the distant darkness. They got closer and the dark shape took the form of an old, beat-up pickup truck with a trailer attached. It was parked between the trees, just off the side of the driveway, and she could make out recent tire tracks under a thin, fresh layer of snow. Meg squinted at the truck's license plate and repeated its sequence of numbers and letters to herself, committing it to memory.

Chestnut brushed past her, moving confidently toward the truck. From the house, Meg heard voices again. It sounded like three different people talking, then laughing. Fear coursed through her. What if they got caught?

But Chestnut wasn't afraid. He skirted the pickup truck, his nose leading the way, and continued past it to a small, rundown barn. It was old and splintered, but it smelled like fresh-cut pine. Chestnut pressed his head against the door, which creaked open.

Meg held her breath, listening for any signs of life.

What if someone was posted guard inside the barn? What if the people inside the cabin heard the door? Nothing changed—the barn was silent, the voices carried on, and Meg heard nothing but Chestnut's breathing. After a long moment, she relaxed. They stepped inside and Meg closed the door quietly behind them. They were left in total darkness, but Meg found herself overcome with a smell so familiar and comforting that it made her feel right at home: the scent of freshly cut Fraser firs.

Meg inhaled deeply through her nose. It made her mad to think of the trees—her family's trees—here, in these dangerous surroundings with these terrible people. Those beautiful trees that her parents and Sarah and Ben had nursed from saplings didn't belong here.

She needed to see them for herself so she could have proof for the sheriff. She reached out in front of her, feeling the darkness for any obstacles. A squarish mass—a wooden crate maybe?—blocked her path. She was just feeling her way around it when she heard footsteps approaching from outside.

Panicked, Meg fumbled her way to the other side of the crate and crouched down behind it. She pulled Chestnut to her and buried her face in his fur. She willed him to be quiet.

She heard the door creak open, and suddenly a bright light shone into the barn, blinding her. It illuminated a huge, hulking shape on the opposite side of the barn, covered in brown burlap. "I told you," a man crowed. "A hundred and fifty trees. We swiped them right out from under that farmer's nose."

Anger bubbled in Meg's stomach. The thieves were bragging about their accomplishments! Like they'd done something remarkable instead of ruining a bunch of good people's lives. She had the urge to rush out from her hiding place and shout at them, to tell them about all the harm they'd done and how selfish they were. But Chestnut pressed his nose into her hand, drawing her attention back to him. His wide, fearful eyes glinted in the light of the man's headlamp. Meg held Chestnut's gaze and stroked his fur, doing everything she could to calm her dog with her presence.

The thief's footsteps echoed as he walked into the barn, and a series of lighter, faster footsteps trailed after him. From behind their crate, Meg could just see the man's arm as he raised the edge of the burlap covering, revealing a pile of freshly cut Fraser firs — direct from Briggs Family Tree Farm.

A woman gasped. "That's a lot of trees, Bill."

Bill laughed. "Sure is. They'll sell like hotcakes too. Mark's already got a buyer." He covered the trees back up. "We're delivering them first thing tomorrow. No muss, no fuss." He brushed his hands together as if he were brushing off some dirt. "Come on. It's cold out here."

When the light had disappeared, the creaking door had slammed closed, and the footsteps had receded, Meg dared to breathe again.

"Chestnut," she whispered through the lump in her throat. "You did it! You found them!" She scratched him under the chin and kissed him gently on top of his head. "I'm so proud of you. I knew you could do it."

Chestnut returned Meg's kisses, wiggling happily.

She spent a long moment rewarding him with affection, but in the back of her mind, she was counting again. She wanted to make sure that the thief had time to get to the house before they opened the barn door to escape. This time she counted to one hundred. "Come on, boy," she whispered. "We need to get home and tell Mom and Dad."

As if he understood every word, he darted around the crate and pawed at the door.

"Shhh," Meg said. "Finding them won't do us any good if we get caught now." She eased open the shed door so it made as little noise as possible, then waited to make sure no one heard anything. Then she and Chestnut quietly tiptoed outside, down the driveway, and back into the woods.

Meg didn't feel the cold anymore. Her muscles didn't ache, and she wasn't shivering at all. Only one thing mattered: Chestnut had solved the mystery and found the stolen trees! Her mom and dad were going to be amazed when they found out. Chestnut might even get an award from the sheriff!

When they were far enough from the cabin in the woods, Meg spoke.

"Come on, boy," she said to Chestnut. "Let's go home."

★ CHAPTER 25 ★

Their tracks through the woods hadn't been completely covered by snow yet, and it was easy to follow them homeward. Meg was bursting with new energy that propelled her forward, and Chestnut seemed to understand that he had done a good job. As he trotted through the woods, he barked and snapped playfully at tree branches and piles of wet leaves. Meg laughed at him, and he ran in a circle around her, kicking up snow in all directions.

Suddenly, the sky opened up, and the light snow-fall became a thick white curtain—a torrent of huge flakes that made it nearly impossible for Meg to see where they were going. Within moments, their foot-prints had disappeared, and she was totally turned around.

Panic overwhelmed her. In every direction, she saw only a carpet of white spreading as far as she could see. They were lost. The cold returned in an instant and sank deeper and deeper into Meg's bones, until she could barely put one foot in front of the other.

Meg stumbled along, hoping for a break in the snow. They were at the top of a hill when suddenly she tripped on a root buried under whiteness and fell facedown. But she didn't stop when she hit the ground —she kept going. Meg slid headfirst down the steep incline, bouncing over rocks and downed tree branches. With an *oof*, she finally came to a stop at the bottom, landing in a curled-up heap. Chestnut bounded after her, barking.

He stood over her, licking her face until she sat up.

"I can't keep this up, Chestnut," she said, pressing her face into his fur. "Maybe we should just dig a hole and sit tight until the snow stops." Her right side was scraped and sore from the rough trip down the hill—but the pain felt far away and unimportant. There was nothing more urgent now than her need to rest.

Meg found a spot at the bottom of the hill where a downed tree and a large rock had created a small nook. She started scooping snow from the narrow space with her hands, and Chestnut joined her. She dug out a shallow hole and packed the displaced snow into a tall pile that curved around them and blocked the wind. The longer she sat on the icy ground, the deeper the cold soaked into her bones. Meg struggled to keep from shivering and fought to keep her eyes open. It was such hard work . . . but eventually a soft, soothing voice in her head told her not to bother fighting. Everything would get better if she just gave in, it said.

The snow was falling so fast that Meg couldn't see the nearby trees. Chestnut curled around her, and Meg drew warmth from his body.

"We'll just rest here until the snow stops, okay, pal?" Her voice sounded far away, even to herself, but she was finally feeling comfortable. Her eyes felt so heavy. Everything felt heavy.

She let her eyelids fall shut.

Something rough and warm scratched across her face.

"What the . . . ?" She opened her eyes to see Chestnut's face close to hers. "Chestnut?" she asked, disoriented. Her tongue felt thick and clumsy in her mouth. Her dog's name came out sounding like *Chusnh*. Her lips were dry and cracked, and her eyes were crusted with snow.

Chestnut licked her face again, and it occurred to Meg slowly that he was trying to keep her awake—but understanding that information didn't help her act on it. She knew she should wake up. She knew that falling asleep out here was dangerous. But now that she was lying down, with Chestnut so close, she felt so toasty and cozy. She didn't want to move. She didn't want to think. It couldn't hurt for her to close her eyes again for just a minute, right? She took a deep breath and sighed, nestling her head against her arm. After a quick rest, she'd be ready to walk the rest of the way home. She just needed a minute.

Thump!

Something heavy slammed into Meg's sternum, knocking the wind out of her. She gasped, opening her eyes. She gulped in a mouthful of air and snow and gagged, searching desperately for her attacker.

Chestnut's front paws were on her chest. All of a sudden he rose up on his hind legs, with his front legs suspended just above her. Then he slammed straight down, dropping all his weight onto his front legs and thumping into her body again—almost as if he was giving her CPR.

She tried to say his name, to tell him to stop, but nothing came out. Her tongue was as heavy as her eyelids. She tried to blink, but once she closed her eyes, they wouldn't open again. That was okay, she decided.

Thump!

Chestnut jumped on her again, but she didn't even try mustering the strength to speak. In her mind, she begged him to just let her sleep for a minute. She had several very good arguments about why it was best for her to rest, but no strength to give them. That was okay, though. Chestnut would understand what she needed. He understood her.

Thump!

Meg's eyes fluttered open. Chestnut nuzzled at her face, at her hand, at her ear. He pressed his head into her, demanding her attention. Demanding she wake up. *Stop it, Chestnut,* she thought. *Please, just leave me alone.* Then, just as her eyes fell closed once more, Meg spotted Chestnut in the distance, growing smaller as he ran away. He was leaving her alone.

Finally, he would let her sleep.

★ CHAPTER 26 ★

The world around Meg had turned to ice. With each step she took, the landscape was even further transformed. Every single Fraser fir on the farm was decorated with a million tiny icicles that sparkled in the sunlight. Before her, a glowing ice cave beckoned, calling her to investigate its hidden depths. She looked down and was surprised to see that she was wearing boots made of ice and snow. Her coat glittered with a thin layer of diamond-like ice that covered it completely.

She heard a sound and turned. A white dog stood before her. She was majestic and radiant. She walked toward the cave and Meg followed her. The dog's footsteps were silent on the crunchy snow, and Meg stared in awe at the tracks she left behind—each one glinting in its perfect form. The dog turned back to make sure she was following. Meg was startled by the intelligence in her blue eyes. She wanted to call out, to ask this beautiful and mysterious creature where she was taking her, but Meg's mouth was frozen. Her tongue was brittle and useless.

Meg took another step into the silent ice cave. The glow of the dog in front of her illuminated the way. The smooth, shiny walls reflected Meg's face a thousand times, and she gasped in surprise. The icy air tightened her lungs and made it hard for her to breathe. It was so cold that it was hard to think. But she took another step.

Where was this dog leading her? Though Meg didn't know where they were headed, she felt compelled to follow. She slipped and slid to keep up with her silent movement. She was glad for the dog's company. If she left her, Meg would be alone in the dark. Ahead, the cave curved out of view. For an instant, the dog was out of sight too, and the cave went dark. Its ice ceiling and walls cracked and creaked. The sound was eerie in the darkness, and Meg hurried along. She had to catch up with the dog.

When she turned the corner, Meg was taken by surprise. The dog had stopped. She was waiting for Meg, her blue eyes serious. Her tongue lolled to one side. Her breath fogged in the frigid air, turning to sparkling crystals that fell to the ground one by one with a series of jingling sounds. When the dog saw her, she barked. Then she leaped toward Meg, licking her excitedly.

"Hey!" Meg said. She was confused. The dog's warm breath tickled her ear. The damp moisture of her tongue heated her face.

"Meggie?" a voice tried to drag Meg away from the ice cave and the beautiful white dog. "Meg! Wake up!"

Meg felt like she was trying to move her body underwater. She sighed as something scratchy and wet rubbed across her face.

"Meggie, wake up!" a firm voice urged her again. Someone was shaking her.

"Meg! Meg, can you hear me?" another voice called out.

Meg tried to ignore them, but the voices were insistent. The warmth wiggled against her until she couldn't ignore it any longer. She opened her eyes, blinking away the cold that seemed to have frozen them closed.

For a second Meg didn't know where she was. She saw dark sky, illuminated by the glow of white snow all around. She saw the tops of the trees towering far above her. And closer in, her mom and dad were bent over her, their faces masked with worry. Meg's whole world swooped terribly, like she was flying in a stunt plane, and she felt queasy.

As Meg tried to focus her eyes, her mom began to cry. Thick tears streamed down her cheeks. "Oh, Meg," she said, her voice trembling with emotion.

Meg tried to reach for her mom, but something heavy and wet was pressing down on her arms. As she became aware of it, it wiggled and shifted on top of her. Chestnut licked at her face happily. Meg struggled to make sense of what she was seeing.

Her dad reached out and scratched Chestnut's head. "He's a good dog, isn't he, Meggie?" he said, his own eyes red-rimmed and puffy.

"What happened?" Meg finally managed to ask. "Where are we?" Her tongue didn't want to cooperate, the words slipping around in her mouth like fish trying to dart away.

Her dad smiled. "Chestnut came to the house. He barked and scratched at the door until he woke us up. When we opened it, he barked and whined and jumped all over me. I had no idea what was going on, so I sent your mom to go get you. I figured you'd be able to understand what was wrong with him. When we saw that you weren't in your room, we realized what he was trying to tell us. Led us straight to you."

"He saved your life!" Meg's mom said, pulling Chestnut in close and crying into his fur.

Meg's dad bent over her. "Come on, Meggie. Let's get you home now."

He wrapped his strong arms around her, lifting her from her snowy bed. "But, Dad," Meg said, struggling against her fatigue. "We found them. Chestnut found the stolen trees." Saying even that much exhausted her, and she slumped against her father as he held her close.

"Is that what you two were doing out here?" he asked. The warmth of his arms and the blanket that her mom laid over her started to bring Meg's body temperature back up. Her arms and legs tingled painfully. She gasped, suddenly realizing how dangerous their adventure had become.

"Let's get you warm and safe first," her dad said, his voice thick with emotion. "Then I'll call the sheriff's deputy. We'll see what she can find out about the trees."

Meg sighed and let her eyes slide closed once more. She and Chestnut had done what they'd set out to do. Her mom and dad would take care of everything from here. The next thing she knew, her dad was pulling the blankets tight around her as she lay in the back seat of his truck, and she burrowed into them happily.

A warm, furry form pressed against her. She opened her eyes to find Chestnut curled against her on the truck seat. He nuzzled her neck with his snout. She breathed in a happy, tired sigh of relief and fell back to sleep, hugging her dog tightly.

Bright sunlight pressed against Meg's eyelids and she fought her way up from a deep slumber. She opened her eyes to find herself tucked tightly in her bed. Heavy blankets, a space heater, and Chestnut lying right next to her made her extra toasty. The dog was snoring peacefully.

As she stirred, Chestnut's eyes opened. He whimpered and sat up quickly, studying her worriedly.

"I'm okay, buddy," she croaked. "I'm really okay. I promise." She was so happy to find her dog in her bed for the very first time. They had accomplished the unimaginable. They'd found the trees, and Chestnut was here with her. He was watching over her—a part of the family, finally.

Meg's parents came into her room and hugged her from either side of her bed. Her dad placed a cup of hot cocoa on her bedside table, and her mom fussed over her, asking if she was warm enough, or too warm, or hungry. Meg was starting to feel guilty.

"I'll get up and get dressed, Mom," she said, struggling against the quilts that swaddled her. "It's sunny out—it'll be busy at the lot." Her throat was scratchy and dry, and she coughed, which made her body ache.

Her mom shook her head. "Not on your life, Meggie. Gigi's on her way to spend the day with you. She'll keep you company—and keep you in bed. You had a close call last night. You need your rest."

Meg slid back down onto her pillows. If she was being honest with herself, she was grateful. Just the thought of getting up and going to the tree lot was exhausting, let alone actually doing it. She sighed. "I'm sorry, Mom, Dad. I really want to help."

"Don't you worry about the farm," her dad said as he kissed her head, then pressed the back of his hand against her forehead to check for a fever. "We'll take care of the farm. You just get strong again."

"We're still going to talk about what happened out there," her mom said. "You should not have gone out there alone, and it is *never* okay for you to put yourself in danger like that. Not for the farm, not for any reason." She sniffled and wiped her eyes. "And we still need to talk about that." Meg's mom pointed to the dog curled at Meg's side, his head resting on her stomach.

Meg sighed. She nodded. "I know." She put a hand on Chestnut's head. "I understand, and I . . . I'm willing to accept whatever you decide about Chestnut."

It was so hard for her to say these words that she started to cough again.

Her mom pushed a lock of hair behind her ear. "Just rest, Meggie. Rest and get strong. You'll be back to normal in no time."

"Are you hungry?" her dad asked for the seventeenth time.

Meg's stomach grumbled in response, and they all laughed. "I guess I am."

Just then, Sarah and Ben burst into her room. Ben carried her downstairs for breakfast. Over pancakes, he and Sarah were amazed by the story of Meg and Chestnut's night in the forest. Ben nearly choked on his food as she told them about finding the stolen trees. Sarah put her arm around her.

"Meg," she said, resting her head against her younger sister's. "That's actually amazing. And you're an idiot for doing something that dangerous. But also seriously impressive. I'm just so glad you're okay."

Meg was embarrassed by their attention, just as she was embarrassed by the fact that she nearly fell asleep at the breakfast table. Her mom took one look at Meg and commanded everyone to leave her alone.

"Go lie down on the couch, Nancy Drew," her mom said. "You look like you're about to fall asleep in the syrup."

Her grandma got there a few minutes later, and Meg's family bustled out the door to go to the lot. When they were gone, Gigi tucked a blanket snugly around Meg and sat on the edge of the couch next to her. "You doing okay, sweetheart?"

Meg nodded, though her eyes were growing heavy again. "Gigi," she said, feeling her throat tighten. "I'm sorry I lied to you about Chestnut."

Her grandma leaned over and kissed her forehead. "Apology accepted, Meggie." She ruffled Meg's hair. "But don't ever do anything like that again. It frightens me so much that something could have happened to you — that I could have woken up this morning to find out I'd never see you again."

Tears stung Meg's eyes, and she didn't fight them. "I won't, Gigi. I promise."

"Good," her grandma whispered. "Then that's that."

She smoothed the blankets and adjusted the pillow behind Meg's head. "Get some sleep, sweet girl," she said, before bending over to kiss Chestnut. "And you too, sweet boy."

When Meg woke next, the house smelled like grilled cheese and tomato soup. Her grandma set a tray on the table beside her. "If you're not hungry, I can put this away until you are," she said.

Meg sat up. "No, I'm super hungry," she said. She was already feeling better, and her throat didn't feel nearly as sore as it had a couple of hours earlier. "Thank you, Gigi."

Chestnut hopped up and ran to the door. "I'll take this guy out while you start your lunch," her grandma said. She pulled on her boots and coat while Meg nibbled at the perfectly crunchy bread and melty cheese. She was finally feeling warm all the way through. This, more than anything, made her realize how dangerous her adventure with Chestnut the night before had been. She felt scared again as she remembered her dream of the ice dog and how cold she had been. Meg finally admitted to herself that she might never have made it back—might never have seen her family again.

But Chestnut didn't let that happen.

When her grandma and Chestnut returned from their walk, Gigi stomped the snow off her boots. "This guy's a special one, isn't he?" She scratched at Chestnut's ears as he wagged his tail against her leg. "I walked him over to the lot, and he ran right up to your dad. Followed him around for about thirty minutes. Reminded me of old Bruiser for a minute there."

Chestnut sat patiently while Meg's grandma wiped the snow off him with a towel, then scooted over to the couch and wiggled his way onto Meg's lap. Her grandma sat down beside them on the couch, and Meg leaned against her shoulder. Meg was overwhelmed with gratitude—for Chestnut, for her family, for everything. She patted Chestnut's belly, feeling his heartbeat against her hand.

"He sure is, Gigi. And he's a hero, in my book."

When Meg dozed off again, her grandma sat reading in the recliner and Chestnut curled up on top of Meg's feet. She didn't know what was going to happen when her parents talked to her about the dog, but she did know one thing. No matter where Chestnut lived, he would always be her dog.

★ CHAPTER 27 ★

The days that followed were a whirlwind of activity. The sheriff arrested the tree thieves. Meg's dad, Ben, and Mr. Mike drove the trailer to the hideout and recovered the stolen trees. A newspaper reporter came to the tree farm to investigate the theft, and Meg's mom told him the story of Meg and Chestnut tracking the thieves through the woods. The next day, a picture of Chestnut sitting in front of the family's Christmas tree was on the front page of the newspaper with the headline THE DOG THAT SAVED CHRISTMAS.

Business at the tree farm was booming. Everyone in town wanted to buy one of the stolen trees and meet

Chestnut. He was a celebrity! Families came to take pictures with him, and Chestnut quickly became the mascot of their tree farm.

While Meg was at school, Chestnut stayed close to her dad's side at work, quickly learning how to fetch things when he asked for them. It made Meg happy to know they spent a lot of time together when she wasn't home. Every time she saw them together, she crossed her fingers.

Colton and Meg noticed that the symptoms of Chestnut's separation anxiety had started to go away since Chestnut found a role on the farm. Sometimes he still got nervous when he had to be left home alone, but they were crate training him. Day by day, it was getting better.

Meg had never seen the lot so lively. Her ornaments were flying off the shelves, especially when people found out that she had made them to try to raise money to keep Chestnut. The woman from city hall came back with her friends and they bought more than two hundred of Meg's ornaments. They happily announced that the name of this year's Christmas display would be "Chestnut's Fir."

During a rare slow moment at the tree lot on Christmas Eve, Meg's mom and dad found her at the cash register. They were red-cheeked from the cold, but their eyes were shining. Her mom hugged her. "Sweetie," she said, holding Meg's face in her hands. "I need you to promise that you'll never do anything dangerous like that stunt, again. Okay?"

Meg nodded. "I know it was a terrible idea, Mom. But I guess . . . I don't know, I felt like I had to do *something*. I just wanted to help."

Her dad reached out and hugged her. "Everything turned out perfectly, Meggie. But if things had gone just a little differently, this Christmas would have been a very different, very sad occasion. We don't want you to risk your safety ever again. If something were to happen to you, Mom and I wouldn't be able to survive it. You and your brother and sister are our whole lives, Megs."

Meg could feel tears building in her eyes. "I

couldn't let the thieves get away with it, Dad. You were going to have to lay off the staff and we might have lost the farm! I knew that Chestnut and I could find the trees and that if we did, everything would be okay." She sighed. "And I had to make it up to you guys . . . all the lies that I told about Chestnut. I had to prove to you how sorry I was."

Meg's mom wrapped her arms around her. "Sweetie," she said. "We know you're sorry. And we forgive you completely. We should have been more open to discussing the whole dog thing with you much earlier." She let go of Meg and looked at Meg's dad. "We were just trying to keep you from getting hurt. But in the process, we forgot to acknowledge how grown-up you're getting."

Her dad cleared his throat. "That being said, we . . . uh, we have something we wanted to tell you."

Her mom's smile grew wider, and Meg's heart began to pound in her chest. Her parents paused.

"We've decided to let you keep Chestnut," her mom said.

"He's a good boy," her dad said.

"And it's obvious that you love each other," her mom added.

"He's part of the family," they said together.

Meg's eyes flooded with happy tears. "Really?" she asked, hugging them both. "Really, really?"

"Really, really," they answered, hugging her back.

Meg couldn't believe how everything had worked out. This was going to be the best Christmas ever!

For the rest of that day and evening, the tree farm was as busy as Meg had ever seen it. After lunch, Meg's dad announced to the family that they had broken a Briggs family record for most trees ever sold, and Sarah high-fived Meg.

"That's because of you and Chestnut, Meggie," Sarah said, grinning. "Nice job."

Ben put his arm around Meg. "Yeah, Micro," he said. "You and Chestnut are like Christmas heroes." He knelt on the ground and scratched Chestnut under the chin. "Plus, it's pretty cool that we're keeping Chestnut."

Ben was right. It was pretty cool, and—even

though her family was still calling her by her nicknames—Meg had never been happier in her whole life. After the tree farm closed for the day, the family headed home to eat dinner and celebrate their successful season. Meg was excited to wrap the special presents she had made for the rest of her family. Chestnut trotted happily beside her. She had her family and her dog, and Christmas was just hours away. All was finally right in the world.

But when they pulled into the driveway, there was a large black pickup parked across it. A man sat on the tailgate, wearing a bright orange hunting jacket. Meg couldn't quite see his face because she was wedged in the back seat between her siblings and Chestnut. But she could tell from his body language that he seemed anxious.

Meg's dad pulled up beside the truck and parked. The family opened the doors, climbing out to see who the man was. As soon as Ben opened his door, Chestnut jumped out of the truck and ran over to the man, barking happily. Something about the way Chestnut greeted this stranger made Meg's stomach turn upside down.

The man jumped down from the tailgate and then knelt in front of Chestnut. He scratched the dog's ears playfully, just like Chestnut liked. As the family approached, the man stood. Meg's head was swimming.

"Good evening, sir. How can we help you?" Meg's dad asked, taking a step forward.

Meg looked from her dad to the man, and then to Chestnut.

"Come here, boy," Meg said. She patted her thighs and looked into her dog's eyes. Chestnut started to stand but hesitated and looked up at the man, like he was waiting for his permission.

Meg felt something drop in the pit of her stomach. Chestnut knew this person, and she suddenly had a horrible realization who he must be.

"My name is Rodrigo Melendez," he said in a deep voice. He held his hand out to shake her dad's. "I saw the story in the newspaper about the stolen trees and

I was so happy to see a picture of Lobo here! I've been looking for him for weeks."

"I—I don't understand," Meg stammered. Her brain was having trouble keeping up.

"Well, you see, Lobo is my dog."

"But he'd been abandoned." When she'd found Chestnut, he was so malnourished and injured that she and Colton had been certain of this. If this man was, in fact, Chestnut's owner, then he must've been the one who abandoned him. Meg's fear twisted into something like anger. Even if he was telling the truth about who he was, there was no way she was going to give up her dog to this man.

Mr. Melendez shook his head. "Of course not," he said. "He was my best friend. Lobo ran off about a month ago, when we were out hunting about fifty miles from here. I've searched high and low, but I was afraid that the worst had happened. That is, until I saw his picture in the paper."

Chestnut licked the man's hand happily, and Meg felt like she'd been punched in the gut. She could barely breathe.

"Mom? Dad?" she managed to say. Her mom put her arm around her and pulled her in tight. Her dad's face remained impassive, but Meg could tell that he wasn't going to give up Chestnut without a fight.

"It's okay, Meggie," her mom said. "Don't worry."

"Do you have any proof that he's yours?" Meg's dad asked the man evenly.

Mr. Melendez nodded, then took his phone from his pocket. "These are pictures I took of Lobo a couple of months ago, when we went hunting up in the mountains."

He handed the phone to Meg's dad, who scrolled through the photos for a long time before handing the phone to Meg without saying a word. She scoured the photos for any sign, any detail that Mr. Melendez had gotten confused. Perhaps his dog had a different white paw, or differently shaped ears. She was certain that if she just looked hard enough, she'd find proof that this man was wrong—or even an imposter. But with each swipe, her heart sank further and further. It was undeniable. These pictures were of Chestnut. And he and

Mr. Melendez had lived a happy life together. Something caught in her throat.

Meg's eyes froze on a picture of Chestnut, his nose pressed happily to the ground, his tail in the air the way he held it when he was tracking. She almost smiled in spite of herself. He really was a great dog. But the sorrow that was building inside her was too much to bear.

Meg nodded, handing the phone back to Mr. Melendez.

"Forgive me," her dad said to the man. "You can understand why we'd want to be sure. Our daughter and Chestnut—sorry, Lobo—have gotten very attached to each other, and now that Lobo's become a local celebrity . . . well, we just can't be too careful."

"I understand," Mr. Melendez said kindly. "I'd do the same for my daughter." He turned to Meg. "He really is a pretty special dog, so I can understand how you'd come to love him very quickly."

Meg nodded, but she couldn't find any words. What words were there anyway for something like this—for the sadness of finally being together with her dog, only to have him taken away from her? It all seemed like some cruel trick. After everything she and Chestnut had been through together, this was how it ended. Not with shelters or robbers or getting lost in the woods, but with this.

She looked up at her parents, desperate for them to give her a reason why they should get to keep Chestnut, even if this man was his former owner. "So what?" she wanted to yell. Chestnut was her dog now. She loved him and he loved her. It was Mr. Melendez's fault that he lost him, and Chestnut nearly died. She saved him. Didn't that count for something?

But her mom just looked at her with sad eyes, and her dad looked away, clenching his jaw.

"Meggie," her mom said quietly. "It's time for Lobo to go home."

Her whole family was watching her, their expressions almost as miserable as hers. Finally, because she couldn't manage to say anything to the man who had come to take her dog away, Meg knelt down in front of Chestnut. She hugged him tightly, then whispered into his ear. "You are the best dog ever. I'm so thankful that I got to know you. I love you, but you belong to Mr. Melendez, and I have to let you go."

Thick tears streamed down her face, and Chestnut turned to lick them away. She hugged him again, then stood, nodding to Mr. Melendez.

"Thanks for taking such good care of him," the man said. "You're a great young woman." He shook her hand. Meg tried to smile at him through her tears, but it ended up looking more like a grimace. Then, he turned and opened the door to his truck. Confused, Chestnut looked at Meg, then at Mr. Melendez, then back at Meg.

"Go on, Chestnut," Ben said, because Meg couldn't bring herself to say it.

Chestnut stayed put, looking into Meg's bleary eyes. He whimpered.

After a minute, Mr. Melendez picked Chestnut up and put him onto the seat of his truck. He closed the door. "Merry Christmas, folks," he said, his voice sounding a little sad. He walked around the front of his truck, hopped in, and pulled away.

As Meg watched Mr. Melendez's truck head down the drive, Chestnut popped up in the cab's back window. He pressed his nose and paws to the glass. He barked loud enough for them to hear, even outside the truck. Meg wondered if she would ever feel merry again.

★ CHAPTER 28 ★

Knock knock knock!

The rapping on her bedroom door yanked Meg from slumber.

"It's Christmas, Micro!" Ben called from the hallway. "You going to sleep through presents?"

Meg sat up. Christmas would help make everything better . . . even the empty place in her bed where Chestnut should have been sleeping. A pang of sadness plucked at her heart, but she pushed it aside. Today, she was going to enjoy the day with her family. No matter what.

As she pulled on her bathrobe and slippers, she could hear her family moving around downstairs. Sarah was laughing at Ben, who was singing, "We wish you a merry breakfast, we wish you a merry breakfast, we wish you a merry breakfast, and a happy brunch, too!"

Then Meg heard the mudroom door open and close. She heard her grandma's voice call out "Merry Christmas, my loves!"

Meg didn't want to miss another minute, so she rushed out of her room and down the stairs, two at a time. "Merry Christmas, Gigi!" she called out, sliding across the wooden floor to wrap her grandma in a hug.

Gigi kissed her head and said, "Merry Christmas, my Meggie." Then she looked at Ben. "Benjamin, will you please go out to my car and bring in the gifts?"

Ben nodded happily, then pulled on a Santa hat and his boots. "Ho ho ho, Grams!" he said as he gave her a hug in passing.

Meg's mom and dad were in the kitchen, and Meg was thrilled to see them in their rumpled pajamas and bed-head hair, wearing big, happy smiles. It felt like a long time since they had been able to relax and enjoy themselves. Her dad filled the coffeepot with water, while her mom set out a plate of muffins and sweet bread. The house began to fill with the smell of coffee brewing. Meg took a deep breath, enjoying this moment with her family.

"Hey," Sarah said, putting her arm around Meg's shoulders. "I'm really sorry about what happened with Chestnut. Are you doing okay?"

Meg nodded, though for an instant, her sadness hit her like a wallop. She pushed it away. "I'm . . . I'm okay. I miss him, and I'll never forget him. But I know that giving him back to Mr. Melendez was the right thing to do."

Sarah hugged Meg close to her. She kissed the top of Meg's head. "You're growing up so fast, Meggie. I'm really proud of you. And you're just about the coolest person I've ever met."

Meg could barely speak through the tightness in her throat. "Thank you," she squeaked as she hugged her sister back. There was a lot she wanted to say to Sarah, about how much she admired her and how much she meant to her. But for now, a thank-you was enough.

Ben carried in the bags of presents and arranged

them under the Christmas tree. He tracked in fresh snow, and when Meg looked out the window, she saw that the farm was coated in a fresh layer of soft, fluffy white. The scene outside their window looked like a Christmas card. Meg loved the farm so much, and she was grateful for another year that she had gotten to spend living there.

Her dad put a log on the fire and took a deep slug of his coffee. "Well, are we going to open these presents or just spend the day staring at them?"

Meg's mom laughed and kissed his cheek. "Merry Christmas, honey," she said. Meg's dad kissed her back.

"Ewww," Ben groaned, but Meg knew that he was teasing. They were all happy to see their parents smiling again.

Once Meg's mom had brought her grandma a cup of coffee, they all sat down around the tree. Ben was grinning. "I get to be Santa this year!"

Their dad cleared his throat. "Weren't you Santa last year?"

Ben started to argue, but Sarah interrupted. "In the name of peace and harmony, I'll give up my chance to play Santa this year." She bowed magnanimously to Ben. "Don't say I never did anything for you."

Meg cleared her throat. "And in the name of peace and harmony, I'll pretend that I'm still a little kid for one more year, so that Ben can be Santa."

"Nah, Micro," Ben said as everyone laughed. "You're too grown-up for that. You go ahead . . . Santa."

Beaming, Meg took the first gift from her brother and delivered it to their grandma. "This one is from Ben, Sarah, and me. Merry Christmas!"

Gigi opened her gift and cooed over the framed photograph of her three grandchildren. "Oh, I love it. Thank you!"

Meg passed out gifts to her parents and siblings, smiling as each one oohed or aahed. Sarah loved the new purse that her parents had bought for her, and Ben was super excited to try out his new basketball shoes. Her parents loved the gifts from their children, and everyone especially loved the special ornament that Meg had made for each of them.

"I think it's time Santa opens a present, don't you?" her dad said, winking at Meg.

Meg sat down and her grandma handed her a large, heavy box wrapped in shiny blue paper with a fancy blue bow.

"Here, Megs. Open the one from me."

"Oh, Gigi, it's so pretty!" Meg slowly pulled off the tape so she didn't rip the paper.

Beside her, Ben groaned. "Slowest. Unwrapper. Ever."

"Shhh," Meg said, grinning. "I like to save it for —"

"Crafts," Ben interrupted. "We know."

When Meg had finally gotten the tape peeled off, she removed the paper to reveal a box with a picture of a sewing machine on it. "Oh my gosh!" she gushed, standing to hug her grandma. "I love it! Thank you so much! I can't wait to learn how to use it!"

Her grandma smiled, her eyes crinkling at the corners. "I thought I could teach you how to sew if you'd like."

"Like?" Meg laughed. "I'd love!"

Ben shoved a squishy package into her hands, wrapped in silver paper. "This is from me and Sarah," he said. "I wanted to wrap it in a brown paper sack, so you'd open it fast. But Sarah wouldn't let me!"

After she gently removed the tape, Meg found a pair of soft purple mittens and a matching hat and scarf. They were the exact same color as her new coat and were decorated with shiny silver stars. "Oh, you guys. I love them, thank you!" Meg hugged her sister and brother, then wrapped her new scarf around her neck. "It's so soft!"

Then her mom held out a small box wrapped in red-and-white-striped paper. On top was a tiny green bow. As Meg took the gift, her dad said, "We know it isn't exactly what you wanted, but we hope you'll like it anyway."

Hesitantly, Meg removed the tape. Beneath the candy cane paper, she found a small black jewelry box. Slowly, she lifted off the lid. Inside, there was only a folded piece of paper.

She looked up, meeting her mom's gaze. Her mom nodded. Meg felt nervous and excited, though she wasn't sure why. She unfolded the paper and stared down at the words in disbelief.

"Are you . . . Do you mean . . . ?" Meg ran out of words, and when she looked up at her parents, they were both smiling broadly.

Her dad nodded. "We're sorry about what happened with Chestnut, and we know how hard that must have been. But we can see now that you're mature enough to handle the responsibility and that you understand the risks involved with giving your heart to a dog. If you still want to, we'll take you down to the shelter and you can rescue a pup that needs you."

"Yes!" Meg squealed. Her heart was still broken about losing Chestnut, but she was so thankful that her parents were finally seeing that she was growing up. No dog would ever replace her first in her heart, but she knew she could love another one just as much. Meg ran to her parents and wrapped them in a huge, grateful hug.

As her dad and Ben worked on making breakfast, Meg, her mom, her grandma, and Sarah took Meg's new sewing machine out of the box and started setting it up. "Do you have any idea what you'd like to sew first?" Gigi asked.

"I'd like to make some new curtains for my room," Meg said, staring at the machine as Sarah read the instructions on how to thread the needle. As her grandma took the thread and demonstrated, her mom stood up and turned toward the mudroom.

"Did you hear that?" she asked.

As Meg looked up, she did hear something. It sounded like . . .

"Chestnut?" she said, jumping up from the floor. "That sounds like Chestnut!"

"Meg, it can't be," Sarah said as she stood up too. But Meg was already running to the door. She heard the barking again and she knew it was true. That bark belonged to Chestnut! She would have known him anywhere.

Meg threw open the door and in rushed Chestnut, panting and excited. He jumped up, nearly knocking Meg down in his eagerness. She knelt down in front of him, hugging his wiggling body close to her. "Oh,

Chestnut," she said, burrowing her face into his fur. "What are you doing here?"

"He must have tracked your scent, after Mr. Melendez took him home," Ben said as he moved to close the mudroom door. "That's amazing, Meg!"

Could Chestnut possibly have wanted to get back to her that badly? Chestnut wiggled free of Meg's arms and gave her whole family warm Christmas kisses—even Meg's grandma. The Briggs family laughed at his excitement.

"We'll have to try to get ahold of Mr. Melendez," Meg's dad said, sighing as he patted Chestnut's head. "You sure are a persistent pup, aren't you?"

Just then, Meg heard a car door shut outside. Sarah looked out the window and frowned. "He's saved you the trouble. He's here."

A moment later, a knock sounded on the mudroom door.

When Meg's dad opened it, Mr. Melendez stood there with a sad look on his face. "I am sorry to bother you all on Christmas morning," he said. "But it looks like my hunch was right."

"Please, come in," Meg's dad said. "Would you like some coffee?"

Mr. Melendez shook his head. "No, thank you. When Lobo took off this morning, I figured he must be heading back here." He looked at Meg, then at Chestnut. He sighed heavily. "I'm starting to think that maybe my Lobo wasn't meant to be a hunting dog, after all." He knelt on the floor to pet Chestnut's head. "I'm starting to think that he's found the place that he belongs."

Meg gasped as the meaning of his words began to dawn on her. "Do you mean . . . ?"

Mr. Melendez nodded, smiling. "If you'll have him, I'm pretty sure that being with you is the only place old Lobo wants to be."

Meg couldn't hide her joy as she looked from Mr. Melendez to Chestnut, then to her parents. "Is it okay?" she asked, almost not daring to hope.

Her mom smiled as her dad shrugged. "Well," he said, grinning, "it would save us a trip to the dog shelter."

Meg squealed, hugging Chestnut tight to her chest. "Thank you so much, Mr. Melendez."

Mr. Melendez stood. "Thank you," he said, scratching Chestnut's ears one last time. "For taking such good care of him."

"I promise that I always will," Meg said. Then an idea dawned on her. "Wait," she said, turning to run upstairs. "There's something I want to give you."

She ran to her room, where she'd been keeping the very first pinecone ornament she had made — the one that looked just like Chestnut. She hadn't been able to bear parting with it, so she had never taken it to the tree lot to sell. But she knew in her heart now that it had always been meant for Mr. Melendez.

Back downstairs, she handed it shyly to him. "I made this, and I . . . I'd like you to have it."

The man smiled as he looked at the pinecone, painted to match Chestnut's brindled stripes. The small glass beads that Meg had glued to the front twinkled like Chestnut's own eyes, and the mouth she'd painted on matched his silly grin.

"That's beautiful. Thank you," the hunter said, holding it up to compare it to Chestnut. "I'm going to take it home and hang it up right now. It'll be nice to have a reminder of this boy."

With a final scratch under Chestnut's chin, he turned to the door. "I hope you folks have a very Merry Christmas."

Meg's dad shook his hand and walked him to the door. As Mr. Melendez turned to leave, Chestnut barked once, and the man turned back, smiling. "You be a good boy."

Chestnut nuzzled against Meg, and she could almost imagine him saying, "I will."

After Mr. Melendez drove away, Meg, Sarah, and Ben put on their winter gear and took Chestnut out to play fetch in the snow. After a few minutes, their mom and dad joined them. As Sarah ran with Chestnut, Meg stood next to her parents.

"Thank you," she said. "You have no idea how much this means to me."

"You're welcome, Megs," her parents said as they huddled around her.

Then Chestnut was there, jumping and barking, begging for their attention. Meg hugged him to her, breathing in his scent. "Merry Christmas, Chestnut. And welcome home."

She stood and threw the ball for her dog, knowing that he'd bring it right back to her—that he belonged with her—and that he was finally home. For good.

★ CHAPTER 29 ★

As the school bus turned onto their road, Meg and Colton were cracking up. Their math teacher had told a hilarious story about getting lost in the Mall of America over Christmas vacation, and they were still laughing about it. When they hit the huge bump just before Meg's driveway, their laughter rang out so loudly that the kids around them turned to stare.

The bus pulled to a halt and Meg stood up. "You should come over to my house today," she said to Colton, who raised his eyebrows. "I've got a surprise for you!"

As Meg and Colton walked down the bus aisle, a girl in the third row gently tapped her arm.

"Hey, Meg," Holly Gardner, one of the most popular girls in school, said. "I really like your new coat."

Meg smiled. "Thanks, Holly." For so long she had dreamed of hearing those words, but now, they seemed so unimportant.

"And your dog." Holly giggled. "He's adorable!"

Meg glanced out the bus window to see Chestnut waiting for her at the end of the driveway. "He's pretty great, isn't he?"

Holly nodded. "I read about him in the paper. What you guys did was awesome!"

Meg blushed and headed for the door, but Holly tapped her arm again. "Do you want to hang out sometime?"

Meg glanced at Colton, who was grinning behind Holly, making a ridiculously goofy face. She smiled back at her best friend. "I'd like that, Holly. Maybe you can come over sometime and hang out with me and Colton. He's got a whole bunch of dogs, and they're all amazing!"

Holly beamed, her smile wide and genuine. "I'd really like that." Somehow, Meg got the impression that Holly had been nervous to speak to her. But that couldn't be right, could it?

"See you tomorrow," Meg said, hopping down the bus steps.

Chestnut was waiting for them with his tail swinging in wide swoops. Meg and Colton chased him across the yard and they all stumbled into the mudroom in a pile of kid and dog, fur and coat, boots and paws. Meg and Colton's laughter mingled with Chestnut's happy little barks. She hung up her gear. "Want a snack, buddy?"

Chestnut danced around the room like a waltzing dog.

He followed them into the kitchen. Colton sat on a stool while Meg went to the fridge.

"So, uh, what's this surprise?" Colton asked.

Meg lingered for a moment behind the door of the fridge, a grin across her face. She pulled out a strawberry pie—her mom's famous recipe, Cool Whip piled high on top—and placed it in front of Colton.

"Thank you for everything you did for me and

Chestnut," Meg said. "Seriously, I couldn't have done it without you."

Colton beamed. "Anytime, Meg the Leg."

"Wait," Meg said. "There's something else." She ran to the mudroom and grabbed the small package that she'd wrapped herself. She'd even woven one of her pinecone ornaments through the ribbon to act as a bow.

"Cool!" Colton said when Meg presented it to him.

Meg giggled. "You haven't even opened it yet." Colton ripped open the package. It was a book about chess strategy. "I figured this might help you talk me out of keeping the next dog I find in the woods."

Colton chuckled. "Or think of a plan for how you can keep him." Colton scratched behind Chestnut's ears. "So, you going to help me eat all this?"

Meg grinned. "With pleasure!"

The two of them quickly tucked into the pie, serving themselves heaping slices. Meg gave Chestnut a few small bites of fresh strawberry, laughing when a spot of Cool Whip got stuck on the tip of his nose, and then poured a scoop of kibble into Chestnut's bowl. He gobbled up his snack while she and Colton savored their own. She was remembering the last time she'd come home from school—to an empty, dogless house. She couldn't believe the difference one furry friend made in her life.

When they were done with their snack, Colton said good night and headed home. Then, Chestnut went to the door and barked. Meg glanced at her backpack, where an essay on the Revolutionary War was waiting for her. But the essay could wait—she could finish it after dark. Some things couldn't wait. Chestnut couldn't wait.

Meg put her coat and boots back on and said, "Come on, boy. Let's go track down some squirrels, eh?"

Chestnut barked and jumped, eager to get outside and into the fresh air. He was the kind of dog that needed to run, to track, to explore. A tree farm was the perfect place for a dog like that, and Chestnut was the perfect dog for a tree farm like this.

★ ALL ABOUT THE PLOTT HOUND ★

★ The Plott hound is a smart, resourceful, and courageous dog that is known for its fearlessness and loyalty. They love to go on adventures, track scents, and get dirty, which is why Plott hounds are often happiest outdoors.

★ When sixteen-year-old Johannes Plott immigrated to America in 1750, he brought five dogs with him to North Carolina, where he settled. For over two hundred years, the Plott family bred these dogs, who were lovingly referred to as "the Plotts' hounds." Eventually, they became known as Plott hounds. Today's

Plott hounds are descended from those five original dogs.

★ Plott hounds have a keen sense of smell and are unusually good at tracking. They are also very intelligent and easy to train. Because of these qualities, Plott hounds have historically made excellent hunting dogs, used to track the scents of big game like boars and bears. However, they are increasingly becoming a more popular choice as family pets.

★ A Plott hound has a strong, muscular build. Plotts are known for their glossy brindled coat, which gives the look of small stripes across the body. Plotts can be anywhere from twenty to twenty-eight inches in height, and the average Plott hound is between forty and sixty pounds.

★ The Plott hound is the only coonhound that is not descended from the foxhound. Though

Plotts were bred in the United States, they actually descend from a German bloodhound called the Hanoverian Scenthound. Of the coonhounds, the Plott hound is one of the strongest and most active breeds, which makes them ideal companions in rugged conditions.

★ In 1989, the Plott hound was designated the official state dog of North Carolina. Since then, the breed has grown in popularity and recognition. Beginning in 2008, Plotts have even exhibited at the Westminster Dog Show.

★ Though they can be quite fierce when hunting, at home Plott hounds are eager to please and incredibly loyal. They often make great family pets and can get along with other animals and children alike. That said, Plotts are best suited for an active household, since they need at least an hour of exercise daily.

Long walks or plenty of space to play outdoors is absolutely crucial for this breed. They are known for their beautiful "baying" bark —a long, low howl—which may or may not sound beautiful to any neighbors close by.

★ Their brindle coats are typically short to medium length and have a smooth, glossy appearance. Since their hair is quite short, they are one of the lower-maintenance breeds. Still, you should brush them weekly and give the occasional bath to keep their coat and skin healthy.

There are a huge variety of both purebred and mixed-breed dogs available for adoption from your local pet rescue. It is really important to think carefully about how your family will care for and interact with a dog, so you can choose a breed that's just right for your household. If you have questions about whether a certain type of dog is right for you, contact a local veterinarian or your local rescue organization, or do a thorough internet search to find the dogs that would fit best with your family. This helps keep more dogs from returning to shelters and will help you enjoy a lifetime of happiness with your pet.

★ ACKNOWLEDGMENTS ★

The American Dog team is Best in Show! Thank you, Emilia Rhodes, Catherine Onder, Samantha Ruth Brown, Julie Yeater, Celeste Knudsen, Kaitlin Yang, Helen Seachrist, Elizabeth Agyemang, and the wonderful design, sales, marketing, and publicity teams at HMH; and Les Morgenstein, Josh Bank, and Sara Shandler at Alloy Entertainment. Trophies for Agility, Herding, Showmanship, and Best of Breed go to Laura Barbiea, Romy Golan, Robin Straus, Katelyn Hales, Hayley Wagreich, the talented Stephanie Feldstein, Kayleigh Marshall, Rosina Siniscalchi, Ryan Dykhouse, and my dear, wise friend Laurie Maher.

These folks might be tired of hearing how much I

love and appreciate them, but too bad. Thank you for everything, Brian, the Goons, Virginia Wing, Geoff Shotz, Xander Shotz, Katherine Mardesich, Kunsang Bhuti, Tenzin Dekyi, Susan Friedman, and Vida the Great and Terrible.

Turn the page for a preview of

★ CHAPTER 1 ★

Julian hunched over his desk, shielding his notebook with his arm. He hoped it looked like he was taking notes as Ms. Hollin introduced the next book the class would be reading. But there were no words on his notebook page, just sketches of trees and lakes and old roads. Julian was trying to recreate one of his favorite maps from memory—an old county map drawn by people who had come to Michigan a hundred years ago searching for Great Lakes treasure.

Julian concentrated on getting the lines just right. He imagined treasure hunters and pirates tromping through town in search of gold. He didn't bother paying attention to the title of the book that everyone in class would be reading over the next month. Everyone except him.

Ms. Hollin called Isabelle and Hunter up to her desk to help pass out the books. The battered paperbacks had probably been read by hundreds of other students. Maybe Julian would get a copy with missing pages, and then he couldn't be blamed for not doing the reading.

He knew he should try to keep up with the assignments, but what was the point? He'd spent his whole life trying to keep up, only to keep falling further and further behind. It wasn't fair. Reading was so easy for other kids, but to him, every page looked like a puzzle with pieces missing. Or worse—like someone had taken five different puzzles and jumbled all the pieces together into one big pile.

Hunter slapped a book on top of Julian's notebook and shot him a smirk before moving on to the next desk. As soon as Hunter wasn't looking, Julian picked up the book to make sure it hadn't smeared his hand-drawn map. That's when he heard Isabelle whisper,

"This is almost twice as long as the last book. There's no way Julian can read it."

"Maybe his mom will read it to him," Hunter whispered back.

"Don't be mean," Isabelle said. But it sounded like she was trying not to laugh.

Julian shoved the book into his backpack without looking at it. He was so tired of the looks and whispers. He was tired of kids like Hunter treating him like he was stupid. He was especially tired of feeling like no matter what he did, reading never seemed to get any easier. He only felt dumber each year.

At least Julian had a name for it now: dyslexia. Over the summer, his parents had taken him to a doctor, who told them that Julian struggled to read because his brain was different from other kids' brains—and that it wasn't his fault.

Not that Hunter cared about any of that.

After the diagnosis, Julian had spent a few days at reading camp—or "stupid kids' camp," as he thought of it—but it all went by so fast that it didn't really help him. Meanwhile all his classmates were outside at soccer camp or going fishing and canoeing in Michigan's clear, cool lakes.

Now that he was back in school, Julian's teachers were giving him more time to do his work, but he still couldn't get the assignments done. And his parents were supposed to take him to see a specialist who could help him, but they'd already spent a ton of money on the camp, and Julian knew the appointment would be expensive too. He was dreading the visits anyway. He pictured himself sitting on a hard-backed chair in a dusty office, staring at the pages of a book while a mean old lady leaned over him and shook her head at his stupidity.

But would an expert even help? Could anyone? Part of him wished his mom would read the book with him—or, even better, for him.

At least English was Julian's last class of the day. He had to survive only ten more minutes; then he could forget about books and get back to his maps.

"For tonight, class—" Ms. Hollin called out above the rustling of notebooks and backpacks and zippers, "just read the first two chapters." She started straightening the stack of papers on her desk and cleared her throat.

Julian felt her eyes on him.

He sank lower in his chair. He knew what was coming.

"Julian, please see me after the bell," Ms. Hollin said, tapping the stack of papers. Julian had a sinking feeling that there was supposed to be one with his name on it in the pile.

A few kids snickered. There were more whispers from the back of the classroom, where Hunter sat with his friends. They loved it when Julian got in trouble for not doing his homework, or for not wanting to read out loud in class—which was all the time.

He kept his eyes on the floor, imagining it curving into a slide that would carry him away from school and out to Silver Lake, where he could swim in the cool water and search for bullfrogs in the marshy grasses along the shore. He pictured himself scooping up a fat bullfrog, only to reveal a gold coin from a lost treasure in the mud beneath it.

But the floor stayed flat and boring, except for a small beetle crawling under the desk in front of him. Julian watched the beetle. He knew he should've done the homework. But it felt endless and dumb, like digging a hole in the rain. Eventually, it was easier to just give up and set down the shovel.

The bell rang, and the beetle barely escaped being squished by the stampede of kids leaving the classroom. The bug scurried toward the wall, where it slipped into a crack in the corner and disappeared. Julian wished he could shrink down and follow it.

"Julian."

He looked up. The classroom was empty, and Ms. Hollin had that expression his parents sometimes got, like couldn't he just try a little harder? Like it was somehow harder on them than it was on him. It was usually followed by a sigh of disappointment that his dyslexia hadn't magically disappeared.

Julian pulled himself out of his seat, slung his backpack over his shoulder, and went to the front of the room.

"Do you have your signed reading log?" his teacher asked.

Julian's heart dropped. Every week he was supposed to track how much time he spent reading at home and have it signed by his parents so he could turn it in for credit. He pictured the school library book sitting on his bedroom floor, a rumpled T-shirt thrown over it so he didn't have to keep looking at the cover. He'd started reading it. But even after a whole summer at reading camp, it took him forever to get through the first page.

His parents tried to help him after dinner every night, but by then they were both exhausted from long days at work and distracted by everything they needed to do the next day. Every night, as they yawned their way through the lesson with him, he had to ignore the sounds of his brother's video games in the next room. Henry blew through his homework in no time at all and had the whole evening to do whatever he wanted. Julian usually wound up pretending that he understood and telling them he would finish reading on his own, just to let them off the hook. Once they went to bed, he was left alone, staring at the page until he gave up.

Julian had known from the first day back at school that this year was going to be another failure. Just like last year.

"Are you sure I didn't turn it in?" Julian couldn't bring himself to admit that he hadn't even gotten through the first chapter. Some of the other kids were already checking out their second book. He couldn't admit out loud that he was a quitter.

Ms. Hollin tapped the stack of papers. "I don't have it."

"I . . . I'm sure it's here somewhere." Julian began rummaging through his backpack. As he dug through the jumble of books and papers inside the dark mouth of his black canvas bag, his chest filled with frustration, tightening like a balloon ready to pop.

Julian had let everyone down. Again. He wished his brain was as good as everyone else's. He swore to himself that he was going to do better . . . somehow.

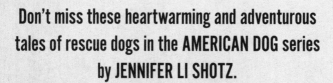
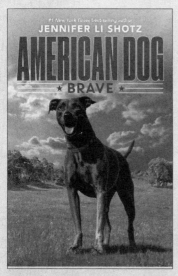
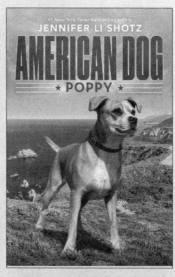
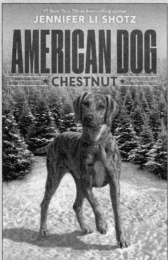

Bianca Alexis Photo

JENNIFER LI SHOTZ is the author of *Max: Best Friend. Hero. Marine* and the Hero and Scout series, about brave dogs and their humans. Jen was a cat person until she and her family adopted a sweet, stubborn, adorable rescue pup, who occasionally lets Jen sit on the couch. Jen lives with her family in Brooklyn, loves chocolate chip cookies with very few chips, and still secretly loves cats. Please don't tell the dog. For the occasional tweet, follow her @jenshotz.